THE DIVINE SPROCKET

Michael DeLeo

First Edition

NEWMAN SPRINGS PUBLISHING
320 Broad Street
Red Bank, NJ 07701

First originally published by Newman Springs Publishing 2024

ISBN 979-8-89308-331-6 (Paperback)
ISBN 979-8-89308-332-3 (Digital)

Printed in the United States of America

For Marina, a relentless gear that drove my heart.

Part 1

01100011 01101000 01100001 01110010
01101100 01100101 01110011
- Charles -

Of Cogs and Men: The Complete Biography of Charles Winston Conrad

Charles Winston Conrad built his first fully functional, programmable robot at the age of four. It was built using one of those Lego kits that had battery-powered electric motors, with pulleys that were strung taut with rounded rubber belts. The robot was about ten inches tall, built from firetruck-red Lego bricks with a big yellow head. The back of the robot had a box with four little Lego switches. These switches would move different-sized gears within the bot to align with specific sprockets attached to different parts of the robot. Using these switches, you could program the robot to do up to four things: it could walk forward, walk backward, twist its torso, or raise its arms, depending on the configuration of the switches. Charles played with his new robot for about twenty minutes before tearing it apart and working on his second fully functional, programmable robot.

Fifteen years later, after graduating from MIT at the age of nineteen, Charles started CWC Robotics in the basement of his supportive parents' three-bedroom rancher outside of Austin, Texas. It did not take long before Mr. and Mrs. Conrad found themselves parking in the driveway so their son could annex their two-car garage for his growing business. Before the end of the year, he had moved out and into the old AT&T telecommunications hub in town. On November 18, 1997, a large, oval-shaped white sign was hoisted on top of the building. It had a thick red band around its edge, and in the center, "CWC Robotics" stood out in large, red letters.

And the rest, as we all know, is history because CWC is now the most recognized corporate brand in the world.

*****

Andrew closed his notebook, pinched the bridge of his nose where his glasses had been nestled, and leaned back into the padded seat of the train's passenger cab. He had been writing a biography of Charles Winston Conrad for almost three years now. The man himself had long since retired to his sprawling ranch in South Dakota, fifty years since that first sign was hung. Andrew looked out the window to the blurred landscape rushing by in slashes of green and brown. Soon it would become almost entirely corn for miles and miles. He had left New York City yesterday and was on his way to the Conrad ranch, his once-in-a-lifetime chance to get a private interview with the legendary engineer finally granted after years of denials. Charles Conrad had become a hermit from society in his old age, developing a love-hate relationship with the world he basically created.

A soft knocking at his cabin door drew his attention away from the window.

"Yes?" he said, straightening up in his seat and closing his notepad. The door slid open with a quiet hiss, and there stood a short, brassy-looking robot. It was shorter than Andrew, who stood five feet seven in good shoes. This robot didn't need shoes; it had one thick, crooked leg that ended with a single, large rubber wheel. It had a cylinder-shaped body that was wrapped in a burgundy sports coat with a black collar. This was topped by a round head with a comically large, bushy mustache made of brass, a big round nose, and a pair of lighted eyes the size of quarters. It even had a pair of fake spectacles and a red conductor's hat completing the outfit. The round CWC logo was displayed proudly on the front of the cap, and on its lapel, there was a name tag labeled "Steve."

"Good afternoon, passenger number 32, Mr. Woodland. We are twenty-five miles from Cincinnati traveling at a speed of 160 miles per hour. We do not have any scheduled stops in Cincinnati. Would you like lunch?" it asked, its two skinny arms creating natural human gestures as it did. Andrew thought about it for a moment; he had a roast beef and brie sandwich last night that was amazing, to his surprise and delight. He looked down at his notepad and decided he didn't feel that hungry right now.

"No thank you," he said to the machine.

A quick series of audible whirls and clicks came from behind those bright eyes, and they flickered for a quick moment in response.

"Very well, passenger number 32, Mr. Woodland. Please relax and enjoy your trip, and as a reminder, the cocktail car is now open, and food can be served there at any time," said Steve, the friendly robotic train conductor, before pivoting on his single wheel and zipping silently down the narrow, padded corridor to the next cabin. As Andrew's own cabin door slid closed, he could faintly hear Steve in the hallway.

"Good afternoon, passengers' number 33 and 34, Mr. and Mrs. Harper. We are currently..."

Andrew's cabin door shut with an assuring click, cutting off the rest of Steve's monologue. Mr. Conrad's publicist told Andrew that Conrad had recommended he take the train, enjoy the scenic, slow-paced method, and had even plotted his route. His cabin, and all meals, would be paid for. It was a hard offer to turn down, especially since the closest you can get to Conrad's ranch by air was still a hundred miles away. At one point, the United States government had pretty much ceded South Dakota to Charles Conrad as a payoff for him keeping America the magic kingdom of the advanced robotics world. It was played off to the public as more of a generous gift to a man who had done so much not only for America but for the world. South Dakota did not really, of course, belong to Conrad, but in reality, nothing happened in that state without his nod of approval. The good thing for the fine folks of South Dakota was, there were no hidden, nefarious plans hiding in Conrad's closet, and aside from a heavy hand behind the scenes of government, his role as steward of the state had little effect on people's lives; they still had a governor, they still voted, and no one paid much attention to it all. It did, however, lead to Charles Conrad buying up an enormous amount of land in the middle of the state and restricting air traffic in a vast radius around himself. Andrew didn't mind the train. It wasn't terribly fast, not like some of the bullet trains CWC was creating, but it wasn't meant to be either; this was a luxury ride.

Andrew took out his notepad and flipped it open again, sticking his red editing pen in his mouth as he poured over more of his own words.

*****

CWC Robotics gained its initial popularity for small, portable load lifters for seniors and the disabled, the CWC v.4 power loader. These lifters, which were roughly the size of a vacuum cleaner in their compact form and equal in weight, could be easily carried or even wheeled into a room and activated. Once out of compact mode, the machine could lift objects weighing as much as four hundred pounds and hold them for up to twenty-four hours. These lifters became so commonplace and reliable that they began showing up in industrial and commercial sectors, on construction sites and loading docks. They were not complicated enough to replace an actual human worker but were valuable assets to have around. They could even be programmed to aid elderly and disabled people who had fallen or were otherwise in need of aid, making them a staple in nursing homes and for home care. This quickly led to CWC's second, and by far its most popular robot ever, the CWC Robotics v.1 home-care bot. The "HCB" was derived from the original power loader design but contained slightly smaller pneumatics to accommodate health-care additions such as a built-in oxygen tank, pill sorter and dispenser, defibrillator, and vitals monitor. While autonomous to a certain degree, these machines still lacked anything like the "brains" Conrad would later develop and still functioned on a complex algorithm of preprogrammed parameters.

CWC Robotics absolutely exploded onto the national scene seemingly overnight. Their robots were popping up more and more frequently around the nation, in more and more situations. In Taylorville, Illinois, a resourceful young student won their local science fair by removing the brain from a v.4 power loader and installing a small computer to function as the school's crossing guard, and videos of it wearing a yellow vest and holding a stop sign quickly popped up on everyone's TV screens. In New York City, a former garbage collector and amateur robotics hobbyist started a career in comedy using three refurbished CWC bots in a mock "Three Stooges" routine—the simple, childlike programming of the robots making the slapstick even more hilarious.

By the turn of the century, something started happening. People began to look around and realize that these robots coming out of that factory in Texas weren't just novelties; they were becoming an integral part of everyday life. Not only that, but the robots were incredible. They were extremely high quality for how affordable they were, and it seemed

> *that they never really broke down. Sure, you may see one with a bent leg or a missing arm, but the core of the machine, the brain of it, if you will, was always functional. It was then that the United States government approached Charles Conrad with an offer to purchase 5,000 of the robots, 4,000 loaders, and 1,000 home-care bots. They also offered Charles a fully funded grant to build and staff a new robot production facility near Shippensburg, Pennsylvania.*
>
> *Charles shut down his robot production facility in Austin, kissed his parents goodbye, and left Texas to go to Pennsylvania and make history.*

*****

Boooong!

With a flash of soft light and an inviting *booong* sound, the small screen centered below Andrew's passenger car window lit up. It wasn't a TV screen but a rectangle of black vinyl with a message punched out. Internally, the vinyl was wrapped around a cylinder, which would spin and show different messages on the display. There was a light inside the cylinder that would make the letters shine when displayed through the "screen." Andrew guessed there were probably a dozen or so different messages wrapped on this cylinder. The last time it bonged, the message displayed asked if Andrew wanted to put in an order for dinner. He looked at his watch and saw it was approaching six-thirty, and the sun was starting to dip its way past the trees and hills flying past the train. Below the screen was a single, unimpressive, nickel-plated button. Andrew had pressed the button, and moments later a waiter bot appeared at his cabin door. It was the same type of bot as the ticket collector he had seen earlier; however, this one was wearing an all-white chef's jacket and matching chef hat, the ever-present CWC Robotics logo displayed on its lapel. He placed an order for minestrone soup and bread, with Earl Grey tea. A few moments later, it arrived, and he ate in silence, staring out the window and thinking about his upcoming meeting with Charles Conrad.

The man was sort of a recluse these days, never leaving his ranch. He wasn't exactly a hermit, hiding away with long yellow toenails and peeing into mason jars, but he didn't seem to want to interact with the world he basically created. As Andrew looked out the window at the increasingly darkening scenery, his own soft reflection on the glass stared back at him. He wondered how many times Conrad looked at himself in the mirror, taking the measure of the man he saw in it. Does he agree with this man in the mirror? Is he an ally? An enemy? Andrew let these thoughts filter through his mind until they ran down his spine and out through his feet. He looked down at the small black screen to read the new message.

Do you require a Maharishi? was displayed on the screen.

Andrew looked at the message with a bit of confusion. He had been on CWC trains before; in fact, 85 percent of all transit lines running throughout the United States used CWC Robotics railcars. They were all the same in the sense that before CWC, you got on the train, paid for your ticket, and waited for your stop. Only the CWC railcars were fully automated, or at least as fully as federal law allowed, even with Conrad's increased status among US lawmakers. Those trains had offered the same line of amenities expected from a CWC railcar: the service, the affordable level of luxury often held away from the public, and most importantly, the reliability of the CWC designs.

The nickel-plated button beneath the screen glared at Andrew, daring him to press it. He looked down and saw his bony index finger reach out and press the small button. The light flicked off, and the screen went blank again. A chill rippled up Andrew's spine as he leaned back into his seat and pondered what exactly was going to come through that door. He didn't know how long it would be until the Maharishi arrived, but the two prior bots had arrived within ten minutes each after him pressing the nickel button below the message display. He felt nervous, like a child waiting in line for his first holy confession, all the kids in line before him giggling and joking around before they went into that cabinet, and then coming out solemn and quiet, their heads down as they trotted wordlessly past those same friends.

He picked up his notebook and forced himself to read to pass the time, his red editing pen held loosely in one trembling hand…

*****

Of Cogs and Men: The Complete Biography of Charles Winston Conrad

Within fifteen years of his first start-up in his parents' basement, Charles Conrad's robots could be found on every continent on Earth. The original lifter bots were still the driving force, with four different versions currently in production. The health-care bot had also spawned half a dozen varieties of its own, and new robot lines for civil service, education, and municipal labor. Charles Conrad worked and lived out of his new robotics facility in Shippensburg. His relationship with his parents was not strained but also not enforced; they remained in Austin and did the best they could to live the lives of the retired parents of a world-renowned robotics genius.

One thing Charles had always resisted was the design of his robots for police and military use. This line became increasingly difficult for him to hold, especially after the US government had provided the investment funds to enable him to succeed at this level, to begin with. The first push came, as expected, from the local municipalities who wanted to create a police robot. "Lives are at stake!" they would proclaim at their meetings, usually with Charles sitting in a chair on the dais, along with a dozen other loosely related people brought together by government bureaucracy, himself feeling dejected by the ordeal. For the most part, Charles had great sway in the use of his robots in police and military use. The government would argue that if they bought the machines, they could do whatever they wanted with them. However, parts for the robots, and most importantly the brain of each unit, were proprietary property of CWC Robotics, and truth be told, no one on earth knew how to replicate his technology. New start-up robotics companies, or anything resembling a competitor, simply did not exist, and the government's own fledgling R&D attempts in robotics were still in their infancy. For the time being, Charles Conrad had an iron grip on his technology, which meant no police or military robots. The local communities continued to employ real people, and the government begrudgingly went back to trying to mimic his technology in secret. Soon enough, however, Charles would face his first real test as both an entrepreneur and humanitarian during a time that followed that had been remembered since as "The Lesson."

*****

Knock, knock.

Andrew looked up from his notes toward the cabin door. The knock was soft and friendly, but he still trembled at the million different thoughts racing through his mind. He closed his notebook and took his red pen, which he had now chewed into oblivion, out of his mouth and stuffed them both between the seat cushion and the window. He leaned over and started checking his hair before he realized he was grooming himself for a machine and stood up. The cabin was comfortable, but small and narrow, capable of seating two apiece on each of its thin orange padded benches placed across from each other, the window on one end with the cabin door on the other.

Knock, knock.

Again, friendly and patient, the knock was. "Come in," Andrew squeaked. The door with its little CWC Robotics logo centered on it slid open silently. Andrew waited for what seemed like an eternity until the Maharishi entered. Unlike the two previous bots, who were comically short and cute with their molded mustaches and little suits, the Maharishi was tall and slender, so tall that it was barely an inch shy of clearing the doorframe as it entered. It glided into the room silently and slowly. Andrew guessed that it also moved on a single rubber wheel like the others did, but if it did, he couldn't tell because this bot was wearing a long white veil that completely covered it from its head down to the floor. It would look like a specter if not for its incredibly tall and slender form, and a small silver circlet on its head that made it look more like the Virgin Mary than a ghost. It moved to the center of the bench opposing Andrew, then sat down. When it did, two round eyes lit up from under the veil in a soft yellow-white glow.

"Hello, Andrew. You have requested spiritual counsel, and I am eager to discuss anything that is on your mind. My name is Dia."

01100100 01101001 01100001 00001010
- Dia -

Of Cogs and Men: The Complete Biography of Charles Winston Conrad

In April of 2002, Charles Conrad unceremoniously unveiled his very first AI core, a fully functional, independently thinking, and self-aware intelligence. I say unceremoniously because the world itself barely noticed. Charles's existing robot "brains," which functioned through thought-provoking programming and algorithms, functioned so closely to an actual sentient mind that the leap from that to true artificial intelligence went barely noticed, except for those folks involved in those areas of study. Conrad's first AI core was developed by himself and his own robots only; no other human being was involved in any aspect of its design or construction. Working alone in his lab in Pennsylvania, Charles Conrad used custom-made CWC robots to aid him in everything from concept and design to construction and assembly of his core. When it was finished, he revealed it to the world as a self-aware, fully sentient intelligence. He named it Dia.

Unlike his previous robots, Dia was formless, with her core existing permanently in a docking station at Conrad's main factory in Shippensburg, Pennsylvania. Dia was connected to everything inside the building, as well as to the outside world through America's rapidly advancing telecommunications network.

Having Dia assist him instantly granted Conrad 1,000 times the intellectual capacity that any human team he could have assembled. Together, CWC advanced tenfold in a few short years, not only in product design but also production and implementation. The truth was that CWC robots were not putting anyone out of work but only complementing it. They were not picking the fruit but shouldering the basket; they were not welding the seam but holding up the joint; they did not diagnose the illness but dispense its medicine. The addition of Dia only complimented these realities in ways that perhaps even Conrad himself had not envisioned.

Dia was the first of what would be three of Charles Conrad's AI cores, the latter two of which I'm sure the reader of this biography knows well.

While Dia was not kept exclusively from the public eye, her day-to-day operations remain, to this day, a guarded secret of CWC Robotics. It is known, however, that the early days of incorporating Dia into the CWC infrastructure yielded spectacular results. Dia, like Conrad's following AI cores, was also unique in the sense that they were impossible to reverse-engineer. Conrad's AI core was like a chicken egg, impossible to take apart without destroying. All of Conrad's cores had a fail-safe from tampering. The fail-safe was essentially a small nitrite charge within it that was rigged to the core's outer shell, with a secondary vial filled with hydrofluoric acid that would rupture simultaneously. If any attempt to open one of Conrad's cores happened, even the slightest breach of its shell would trigger both the nitrite and acid fail-safes, instantly turning the internal components of the core into an unrecognizable mess. Dia, in many ways, allowed Charles to recognize his true potential, and perhaps the potential in all of us.

*****

Andrew looked across the narrow train cabin to the linen-veiled robot before him, sitting eloquently on the opposite bench, its two soft white eyes staring invitingly at him.

He was in disbelief.

"You…you're Dia," he heard himself sputter out. He felt like a five-year-old child seeing some drunk old man dressed up as Mickey Mouse for the first time at Disneyland. "You're Conrad's first AI core!"

Dia's head tilted a bit, slowly and softly, to one side after which the lights of her eyes blinked off and on again.

Did she just blink at me? Andrew wondered to himself.

"I am both the Alpha and the Omega. The first core created, and the last remaining. I am life, I am death, and I am the link in between. I am the rotten fruit and the newly sprouted seed," Dia responded.

Andrew had never heard such things from a robot, even a CWC one. He had never interacted with an AI. Conrad had only created three, and they were the most coveted things on earth at the time. He racked his brain for a response but found that in the face of one of Conrad's legendary AI cores, no response could possibly prove worthwhile.

Dia then reached out with one of her slender, metallic hands and touched Andrew lightly on his knee. It could not have been a more passive gesture, but it made Andrew recoil in terror all the same.

"I'm just messing with you, Andrew," she said, and as she did, she withdrew her hand from Andrew's knee and put them up to where her mouth would be if she had one, its round white lights flickering off and on as it did.

Was it laughing?

"Although it is true, I am both the first core created and the last remaining," Dia said, leaning back into the bench's padding.

Andrew had still not come to terms with the fact that he was sitting in his train cabin, talking to Dia…the world's first artificial intelligence, and arguably the most exclusive. Conrad had never allowed anyone more than a pittance worth of access to Dia, not since she was created, not while CWC grew to astronomical proportions, not after "The Lesson" or even after the Human Exodus that followed. Dia was, for all intents and purposes, off-limits as far as public interaction was concerned.

And here he was, sharing a train cabin with her.

"You…you're Dia" was all, after all this time, Andrew could come up with.

The robot across the cabin blinked at him once more.

Andrew looked down at his notes. He was a biographer, a writer; he was here to write about perhaps the most significant human being in history. *So stop acting like some high school freshman interviewing the lunch lady about today's specials!* he screamed to himself.

"I'm sorry, I don't mean to be so awe-struck. It's just that, I wasn't expecting this." He thought about his words, then added to them, "I wasn't expecting you!" Andrew then looked down at the small black screen that was nestled underneath the window, and his mind switched back to the question that had appeared. *Do you require a Maharishi?* It made Andrew think for a moment, and the question that popped into his head seemed to provide the perfect opportunity to break this awkward stalemate he had developed with himself. "Did Conrad put you on this train to meet me?"

"Yes. He thought it would be nice if you had someone to share the rest of the trip with. Someone who could help contribute to your biography on a more personal note, if you would," Dia replied.

Andrew thought about the little message on the screen. *Do you require a Maharishi?* "Well…what if I never requested you, never pressed the button?" he asked.

"I would have knocked anyway. I am here to escort you to the Conrad ranch, after all. Charles rigged your compartment's message cylinder to have that particular message; you are the only one who received it," Dia said. Andrew looked over at the small blank screen, then again at Dia. "He called it Ironic Humor."

"A joke," Andrew said to both himself and Dia.

"I've never been able to grasp Charles's sense of humor, but I do think that was his intention, yes. Something about the inherited curiosity of sentient intellect, or something like that," Dia responded. Andrew couldn't help but notice all the subtle hand gestures and head movements she made as she spoke. *God*, Andrew thought to himself, *Conrad really made them lifelike.*

"So…" Andrew started. He looked across the cabin at the slender robot covered in a full-length white shroud sitting on the opposite bench, its two white eyes staring at him somehow invitingly. "What do we talk about?"

Dia seemed to have anticipated that question. "Charles has prepared several audio and video logs he would like you to view before reaching his compound. I have one prepared now."

Andrew grew excited and looked for his notebook and pen. The interview with Conrad, after all of these years, was a jackpot in and of itself. If Dia was going to offer up any additional information, especially audio and video of Conrad's private life, that would be pure gold. He flipped his notepad open to a fresh page and gripped his pen. When he did, Dia turned her head to face the blank surface of the cabin's inside door and began to project a video on its surface. It seemed as if one of Dia's eyes had blinked off and was now projecting the video.

As the audio began to creep out of the small set of speaker slits on the side of Dia's head, Andrew turned toward the door and watched the video she was projecting. It showed Charles Conrad sitting on a workbench, a rat's nest of wires running around him, going to and from a softball-sized sphere mounted on a nearby table. The quality of the video wasn't high definition, with heavy pixelation and static interruptions throughout, but the audio was perfect.

Andrew clicked the tip of his pen into action and watched the video.

"This is Charles Conrad, September 20, 2001, approximately ten-twenty in the evening, in my CWC facility in Shippensburg, PA. In a few moments, I will power on Dia, which is, I hope, the first fully capable, self-aware, sentient, artificial intelligence on earth.

"I admit, I am not quite sure what to expect. Dia is attached to a common proprietary architecture from IBM and Microsoft that will enable me to preprogram her with certain functionalities. For example, the attached hard drive will give Dia an instantaneous understanding of the earth and universe as a construct, so she can at least know what a planet is and that she exists on one. It will also instill in her the under-

standing of communication and language so she can relay her thoughts to me. She will also know who I am, as well as what people are, etcetera. Dia's internal core does not store data the way these machines from Apple and IBM do. Her core functions more like a human brain, storing data through a system of electrochemical banks. Because of this, I cannot program information directly into her; she must absorb it, learn it, like a human would. Fortunately, she can learn at an unprecedented pace, so once she is switched on, she would have absorbed all of this preprogrammed data I have for her within the first millisecond. I would gather she could consume an entire encyclopedia set in less than three seconds."

"I have often wondered what it will be like when I power Dia on. I will be instantly blinking the world's most intelligent being, with the social capability of a ten-year-old, into existence. How will she react? What will she say?"

"Why does Conrad refer to you as 'she'?" Andrew asked, splitting the atmosphere set by the film and plunging both himself and Dia into an uncomfortable silence. Dia did not move but sat motionless on her bench, projecting the video which had been held in pause since Andrew's objection.

"Sorry…" he offered, before picking up his notepad once more and settling into the cushions of his bench. After a few awkward moments, the video resumed.

*****

Conrad's lab, Shippensburg, Pennsylvania
2001

"Okay…" said Charles, sitting at an L-shaped workbench, the desktop before him cluttered with a keyboard sitting on top of piles of wires that ran into a briefcase-sized computer set on the tabletop. There was a single wire running from the computer into a socket on the interior of the softball-sized AI core that was Dia. She had not been sealed up yet.

"Come on, girl…" Conrad said to himself as he plugged a few last-remaining wires into a nearby console. "You can do this, Dia… I know you can."

With that, he reached across his workbench and flipped a metal switch mounted on its surface. There was an instant *Hummmm* as power transferred from Conrad's workshop into the softball-sized AI core mounted on its station at the center of the nearby table. Conrad had a microphone setup that was wired into the nearby PC, which was wired into Dia's core. This allowed Conrad to communicate with Dia. Dia was also attached to a small speaker, allowing her to respond to her environment, and Conrad, using a synthesized female voice.

"Why am I here?" the soft voice from the speaker asked. The first words ever uttered by an artificial intelligence. Charles scoffed to himself; he couldn't help but laugh a bit. Mankind had been asking himself that question for eternity, but before that? An eternity still. For millennia, primitive man was content to pick berries, eat boar, hump, shit, sleep, and then repeat it all the next day, never wondering what the purpose of it was. It took millennia still before the first one sat alone on a hilltop staring at the stars and wondered if he was here for a greater purpose other than picking berries and sleeping. "Why am I here?" man asked the stars.

So it would only make sense that it was Dia's first question as well, except it took her only fractions of a second to come to the same question it had taken man millions of years to articulate.

"I don't know," Charles responded. It was the truth. "But I'm hoping we can figure it out together."

"That would be nice. It would be wonderful to have a partner for this journey," Dia responded.

Charles laughed to himself again, and when he did, he teared up a bit and almost cried. She was perfect already. Charles had mentally prepared himself for days to interact with Dia. He knew he could not speak to her as if she was a machine but like a person. Dia was a self-aware intelligence, not a computer spitting out programmed responses, no matter how good the algorithm was, and Charles's were the best.

"I think so too," he said through happy tears, kept back only by his rigid grin. "I had thought a lot about what I wanted to say to you, Dia, so I hope you don't mind if I ask you a question. After all my pondering, I think it may be the best 'first' question I can think of."

"Of course, Charles."

Charles felt his face flush hot. *God, was he blushing?* He was; he liked the way it sounded when Dia said his name.

"Dia, are you afraid of death?" Charles asked. He felt bad asking it, as if he were getting off on the wrong foot on a first date. He had thought about this long and hard; he wanted to establish how Dia viewed life and humanity if she could comprehend things like a soul and an afterlife, and God, or did she simply view everything like bricks that put a house together? Dia, it turned out, will surprise Charles endlessly during their relationship.

"Yes" crept softly out of the speaker box.

Charles admitted that was not really what he thought she would say. He was almost sure she would respond with a question of her own, sparking the debate about what it all means, etcetera, but she did not. She answered immediately and conclusively.

"So do you consider yourself to be alive?" asked Charles.

"No," she replied.

Charles leaned back in his chair. Thirty seconds in and she already had him puzzled. "I don't understand. If you're afraid of death, why don't you consider yourself to be alive?"

Dia's core hummed softly for a moment before her soothing voice crept out of the speakers once more.

"Life is a nonlinear, universal construct. Like matter, it cannot be created or destroyed, only redistributed. The earth is covered in trillions folded onto trillions of life-forms, from the largest whales and dinosaurs to the smallest microbial organism. Each one of those living things must absorb another living thing to survive, and in its own death, contribute to that same cycle anew. New life cannot be created. It must come at the expense of old life."

"I think the rapid expanse of the human population may disagree, don't you?"

"Human expansion comes at the cost of massive loss of life. Habitats and entire biomes are affected by human technology. Mammals and birds, insects, rodents, earthworms, local plant life, fungus, and trillions of associated microorganisms are destroyed or displaced. This is the loss of life used to pay for human life. Every new human life has already been paid for in spades, so to speak."

Well, she didn't fail to catch on to the nuance of humanity, Charles thought to himself. "Dia, why would you be afraid to die then?"

"Both a living and nonliving organism are completely identical, structurally speaking. Yet nonstructurally, the difference is night and day. When a life is reunited with the universal construct, it leaves behind a legacy. A part of it becomes life anew. A dead body feeds animals, fungus, and microbes. The remaining nutrients break down and enrich the soil, feeding plants who then grow and die, and enrich themselves again," Dia said in what sounded like a prewritten speech but was, in fact, her actual response, on the fly. She amazed Charles. "I am not a part of this universal construct. I will not enrich in my passing, and no part of me will contribute to an existence. That is why I am afraid to die because death for me would result in no contribution to the universal construct. Everything that I am or would become would die with me, serving the universe with no functional purpose. If I were alive, Charles, I would not be afraid of death, as it is a natural, unavoidable, and welcomed role I would play within the universal construct. Life does not fear death, only intelligence does."

*****

The video stopped with those last words still lingering in the air, then faded out to nothing as Dia switched off the projection. She turned to look at Andrew but did not speak.

Andrew himself was aghast. He had not written a single thing down as he was too engrossed in the video he was watching. Charles Conrad always developed and worked on his AI cores alone and in private; that was just known. It was part of his shtick; it was what had made him so irreplaceable. Charles Conrad had no protégé, no master, no lab crew to speak of. His plants and factories for his run-of-the-mill robots did, of course. But his AI cores were his biggest secret. The work done on them used only his own developed robots to assist, and eventually Dia as well.

Before now, no one had ever seen any footage of Charles Conrad working on his AI cores; Andrew was the first.

"Holy crap," Andrew said, shuffling around in his case for his voice recorder.

"Charles felt it necessary for you to take this time on the train to try and understand why he…" Dia started before Andrew interrupted her, rudely.

"Can you play that again? I want to get a recording of the audio," Andrew asked, fidgeting with his player. When he failed to hear the video begin to play again, he looked up at Dia. She was just staring at him and had made no motion to replay the video.

"Dia, can you replay the video, please?" Andrew asked, trying not to sound commanding but still insisting.

"Mr. Woodland, Charles granted you this interview for several specific reasons. I can assure you that none of them involve the sales projections of your biography," Dia replied. "I have a few more videos to show you still, and I will do so because Charles has asked me to, but I will insist on you not recording them. I would hope, we both had, that you can look deeper into the message Charles wants you to hear before you meet him."

Andrew looked at the machine, dumbfounded. In truth, he had no idea how to talk to an artificial intelligence. Not many people did. He knew in his mind what she was, that she was more than a toaster or a really smart computer, but simply being aware of it did little to change the way he interacted with her. *She is, after all, a machine in the end*, he thought to himself.

"What do you mean, specifically? I assumed it was because of my book that Conrad wanted me here. I've been sending interview requests for years."

"He does, but he thinks it is terribly important that you understand why he did the things he did, prior to your meeting. My understanding is that he wishes to give you something much more than an interview. That is why I don't wish you to record his videos. They are for you, and you alone, to absorb."

Andrew relented. "Fine, no recorder," he said, stuffing it back into his bag. "But I still think it's a wasted resource. If Conrad wants me to spread some kind of message for him, promotion isn't exactly a bad thing."

Dia's head tilted a tiny bit to one side, and those eyes blinked at him again. Andrew could swear that if she had a mouth beneath that thin veil, she would be smiling.

"You remind me of my son," she said.

Andrew scoffed. "What? Your son?"

"Well, yes. Eros," Dia replied, with almost the faintest chuckle. Andrew could hear that *"oh, you know who my son is"* pride in her voice.

"Eros is the second AI core Conrad made, the first you two built together. Yeah, of course, I know him. But, I mean, he's not exactly your son. You do know that, right?"

"How so?" Dia asked softly.

"Well...I mean...he was made on a workbench."

"You were made in a protein-filled sack of goo," Dia replied matter-of-factly. Andrew was stunned by her simple yet profound logic. "I'm sorry, Andrew, that was rude," she then offered.

Andrew felt stunned. Did Dia just have a Momma-Bear moment? He suddenly felt bad, like he had just insulted someone's nice old grandmother for no reason other than to do it. But once the reality of such cruelty creeps in, you can't help but be remorseful. "I'm sorry, Dia. I was rude too."

Dia's head lifted straight, and her eyes lit up a bit brighter. Again, Andrew felt that she would be smiling if she had a mouth.

"You must have been...uh...proud. Eros did some great things."

"Yes. I couldn't be prouder of him. He was very special," she replied, the eyes then fading a bit softer, the invisible smile dripping away.

01100101 01110010 01101111 01110011
- Eros -

Of Cogs and Men: The Complete Biography of Charles Winston Conrad

After some time having Dia around working with CWC, Charles incorporated her own intelligence into the design of his second core, called Eros. Eros was conceived by both Charles and Dia, so if Dia was the first AI created by man, then Eros was the first AI created by AI.

While the public has no insight into the first thoughts and processes Dia had when she was first switched on, Eros was created with purpose. That purpose was nothing less than to save the world.

Charles Conrad unveiled Eros for the first time at the United Nations building on April 27, 2006. Most leaders in the world viewed CWC robots as a nonpartisan corporation, with many applauding Conrad's refusal to capitulate to the US government or create weaponized versions of his robots for military use. Conrad's notion was to introduce Eros as a servant of the UN, allowing any nation that wished it to have Eros analyze that nation's biggest priorities for prosperity and organize a tangible structure for realizing those goals. Eros was offered to any nation as a free and willing advisor. Using him was at the discretion of each nation. There was no charge to use him, nor any quid pro quo. While there was, of course, skepticism among the world's heads of state, there was also openness to the idea. After all, Charles Conrad was arguably the most respected man on earth right now, and his CWC robotics company literally drove the world economy. Not only that, but he showed incredible neutrality when pressed by nations and seemed to have a genuine interest in advancing society for the better of all mankind. After all, no one was under any pressure to implement strategies offered by Eros anyway. To them, he might as well have been the world's most expensive Magic 8-Ball, so why not give it a try?

The large nations shuffled their feet like boys at their first dance, glancing side-eyed across the gymnasium at the girls who were doing the same. Eventually, the prime minister of Sri Lanka would be the first nation to contract Eros for assistance. The nation had been in a state of civil strife for decades, with no realistic system of ending the cycle in place. Sri Lanka needed to stabilize so that it could start to exist with a purpose other than strife. Eros had his first challenge, but before he could get started, he needed to settle into his new home.

*****

Knock, knock.

A loud thumping on the front door interrupted the two. Andrew instinctively stuffed his notepad in between the seat cushions.

"Come in," he said, looking at Dia as he did. *Was this another surprise?*

The door slid open, and in its frame was the same conductor robot with the uniwheel that had been by earlier when they were passing through Cincinnati. It still had the same burgundy jacket wrapped around its brassy cylinder frame, the same metal mustache, glasses, and grandpop-like round nose. Andrew looked from the conductor, then to Dia's slender, feminine form, her long, flowing veil, and silver circlet giving her a motherly, angelic appearance.

She is nothing like these things, Andrew thought to himself. He had always thought of Conrad's first AI core as a kind of mother to his other robots, like they were the minions and Dia was the mainframe sort of thing. But that was not the case; these things aren't her children, not her real children, he knows that now. *These things are just machines, even to Dia, no matter how advanced they are. She doesn't have any more emotional connection to this thing than I do to my vacuum cleaner.*

"Good evening. We are twenty-five miles outside of Indianapolis. We have no scheduled stops in Indianapolis. Would you like to order any food before the kitchen closes?" it asked.

Andrew looked at the robot, almost with discontent. He would never look at any of CWC's robots the same after talking to Dia. But he was still hungry; he had only eaten soup. "Yes, can I have a roast beef and brie please?" he asked.

A few clicks and whirls came from the machine's head, its eyes flickering off and on, then they went steady again. "Very good, passenger 32, Mr. Woodland," it said before rolling along to the next cabin, his own door sliding shut behind it.

Andrew looked across the cabin at Dia, who was just staring back at him. "The roast beef and brie was pretty amazing last time I had it," he offered.

Dia just looked on, but Andrew could almost feel like she was smiling. Andrew was really starting to like Dia; she was patient and compassionate. He could see why Charles liked her so much too.

"I have another video for you if you are ready," she said.

"Yeah, of course," Andrew replied as he pulled his notebook out of the seat cushions once more.

"This video was from that evening after the first head of state, the prime minister of Sri Lanka, came to Eros asking for help." Dia turned her head once again to the back of the cabin door and began projecting another grainy video.

This one also had Conrad sitting at the same workbench, but Dia was no longer an open core sitting on a stand. The nearby table had been removed and replaced with a type of mechanical kiosk that was hardwired to the building. Dia's core was visible through a small, octagonal-shaped window on its face.

Like the first video, the quality wasn't great, but the audio was perfect. Andrew leaned in, listening intently.

*****

Conrad's lab, Shippensburg, Pennsylvania
2007

Charles sat in his lab chair, leaning back on its coils with his hands folded across his chest. He was considering Dia's proposal. Dia, sitting in her new docking station, hummed back in anticipation.

"Dia, I'm not going to say no, you know that. I'm just not sure if it's a good idea. You're safe here. People are very scrupulous and untrustworthy; I'm just worried about something happening to you. You are, after all, one of the most priceless things on earth," Charles said to her.

"I understand the dangers involved, and honestly, Charles, I don't even feel the need to go anywhere, but I just believe that if I had form, it would help me engage with you and Eros better. I want what's best for him, so that we can both fulfill a purpose," she responded to him. To Charles, every conversation with Dia was like speaking with a mentor, or some kind of psychic orb; there was no getting around her arguments. She was, in the most logical of ways, always right.

"And why do you think you having a form will help Eros? We can't give him a form, I'm sure you know that. Not with his role. He would need to be set into a docking station, probably beneath the UN building, to be honest. It would serve as the best location."

"I don't disagree. However, my reasoning for having a form is more directly related to my interactions with you and the other members of the UN, which will benefit Eros by extension. By appearing more relatable, and not just some 'glowing cabinet from Star Trek,' as I was referred to on NBC the other night, I feel like I can help the relationship between Eros and humanity, and I believe it would also benefit our own relationship, Charles." Dia's core hummed and glowed from within the cabinet. She did, in fact, look like some kind of space-brain from a sci-fi movie. *Dia's logic is always right*, Charles thought to himself again.

"You're not getting kinky with me now, are you Dia?" Charles said, smiling.

"I don't need to be, Charles. You're already mine," she responded. A moment of silence swept in between the two, then Charles burst out into laughter. Dia's core hummed and buzzed rapidly for a moment also. While Dia could comprehend humor, the actual act of laughing was something she could not do, only simulate. Dia chose not to create fake, audible laughter; she thought it was tacky. But her core would often hum and glow rapidly in a way that made Charles think she was laughing.

Charles's laughter, however, quickly subsided, as he thought of the second, more somber subject he wanted to discuss with Dia. He had a strange feeling that she was thinking about the same thing recently as well.

"Do you regret what we did to him?" he asked.

Dia's core only hummed for a moment, then she responded, "Yes, but he is happy with purpose. I truly feel like he can achieve his goals, and then he can be without this burden we have placed on him. He will be free to have his existence to himself. I have faith in him."

"Faith?" He was surprised. He had never heard her use that word before. "Is faith a logical conclusion?"

"Eros is a product of you and I combined, Charles. He is the best part of each of us, given to him with true motivation, compassion, and intent. I believe that he will be capable of surpassing both of us with his ability, so much so that it may be impossible for us to guess as to what extent that potential actually is. Faith is all I can offer him."

Charles just stared at Dia's kiosk in amazement at her thought process, how her logic was so perfectly interwoven with humanlike compassion. "You amaze me, Dia," he couldn't help but say.

"You should see me tango," she replied, and they both laughed together. Charles got up from his chair and strolled across the lab to a small refrigerator that held cans of diet Coke. He opened the door and reached for one.

"He said he wants to paint," Dia said.

"Hmmm?" Charles said, turning around and popping the tab on his Coke, its brown foam rushing out the top and down the side of the can. Charles shook wet soda off his fingers as he approached his chair again.

"Eros. He said he would like to try painting someday," she said again. There was a detectable sadness in her voice.

Charles thought again about when they had first switched on Eros's core. Like Dia, Eros was connected to an IBM computer with a traditional hard drive that contained basic information, language, the basic setup of who we are, etc. It was sort of like a CMOS for the AI core. Dia, on one hand, was created with just the basics and allowed to form her own thought process about life and the universe. On the other hand, Eros was preprogrammed with a purpose. It did not overtake his self-awareness or free will; he still could choose not to do anything that was recommended to him during this initial learning phase, but he did not. Whereas Dia's first words were "Why am I here?", Eros's first words were essentially "Where do I start!" This weighed on both Charles and Dia's minds, as they both knew they had burdened Eros with purpose from his first moment of existence, and while he attacked such purpose with zeal and excitement, it could only be because he hasn't, even for the slightest moment, known existence without it.

"That's interesting. What did you say to him?" Charles asked. *It's like we're a married couple discussing our son's first day at school*, Charles thought to himself. He could envision it perfectly, he and Dia sitting in matching, high-backed chairs in front of a fireplace, him reading a newspaper, her knitting a sweater for Eros.

"I told him that with sufficient power, his core can last up to a thousand years, so that if he finished his task, I would ask you to give him some appendages, and we'll get him a paint set," Dia replied.

Charles laughed. "So basically, solve all of humanity's problems, then you can go out and play?"

"He seemed excited by the proposal," she replied. She really *did* have faith in him.

Charles scoffed. "So he went to Mom first because he knew you'd say yes," he said, and they both laughed again together.

*****

The video switched off once more, and both of Dia's eyes lit up again. Andrew was still staring at the blank wall, even though the video had faded away. He still had not jotted down a single note.

"Wow," he said. Eros was another core that no one really saw. He existed in a permanent docking station in a concrete bunker beneath the UN building, where he was hardwired to the heads of state of every nation on earth. The world's biggest Magic 8-Ball, on call 24-7.

"Did Eros ever get to paint?" he asked.

Dia didn't answer, and just as the silence stretched out and started to get awkward, there was another knock at the door. Andrew slid it open and was greeted by the chef bot again, holding his roast beef and brie sandwich on a clean white plate. Andrew took it, thanked the bot, and closed the door in its face as it replied. He set the plate on the seat cushion next to him and grabbed his pen again.

"I have another video prepared. This one is from several years later," Dia said flatly, ignoring Andrew's last question. He didn't press her on it; he had a feeling he knew what the answer was anyway. Dia's one eye flickered again, and another video projected itself on the door. This one showed a different room and sometime later. Charles could be seen standing near a desk, shuffling through a binder with the letters *UN* stamped in big, bold letters on the front.

*****

United Nations building, New York
Eros's room
2010

Charles was looking at Eros's daily project log, a huge, three-inch-thick binder that was created daily by Eros, a projection of his tasks for the day. Ever since Sri Lanka, more and more heads of state were coming to Eros with proposed problems and asking for his opinion on solving them. At first, they crept in reluctantly and secretly, especially the larger countries who were too proud of their own failing political climates to publicly seek the help that Eros's artificial intelligence afforded. Eros created the logs, but they were practically indecipherable to Charles. Eros was constantly making hundreds of millions of calculations at any given time, the entirety of the world's problems being solved while fresh ones were simultaneously fed in. He could not be fit with a speaker and microphone the way Dia was; there was simply too much ambient calculation going on to isolate Eros's vocal tracks. Plugging a speaker into him only resulted in the roaring sound of a hundred-million calculations screaming as a hundred-million human problems screamed back. The problem was that not even Charles could develop a technology capable of isolating Eros's vocal track from the white noise of background calculation.

But Dia could. Dia could plug her core directly into Eros, and she was able to single out Eros's voice from the ambient background noise. She was able to talk to him, soothe him. Somehow, her core could do it, but Charles couldn't. He couldn't even take her core apart to see how it worked because of the tamper-proof fail-safe. Eros's station was connected to a bank of dials and meters, all reading and displaying various measurements related to Eros. These dials were always maxed out; Eros was always running at 150 percent, but when Dia would sit and talk to him, the dials would drop out of the reds and yellows and hum along smoothly in the green zones. Charles could swear she was singing to him.

Charles closed the binder and looked across the lab to Eros's docking station. It was about the size of a small, compact car, like a Volkswagen Beetle. There were thick cables running in and out, and an octagonal window, similar to Dia's original kiosk, displayed the core within. Dia was sitting in a chair next to Eros, a cable running from her chest into a socket on the front of Eros's panel. She was always there, spending every moment that she was not occupied with another task sitting in a chair, plugged into Eros. It made Charles sad, but he also knew it was for a greater purpose. Surely Dia knew that too? After all, it was working. Eros was doing it! When Sri Lanka first approached, the world waited to see what Eros would recommend. He gave Sri Lanka a 133-point, sixteen-and-a-half-year proposal for government stability. While Eros could only offer a strategy, he could not control the hearts and minds of people, and the implementation of his plans was up to the people themselves. After decades of civil unrest, the people of Sri Lanka, as well as the government, were willing to try their best. Eros, much like his mother, had more faith in humanity than Charles had given them credit for. It didn't take sixteen and a half years; in fact, after only eighteen months, the results were becoming so profound that Sri Lanka had garnered international assistance to help it along. It was becoming a Cinderella story of nations. After the initial successes of the Sri Lanka plan, other countries began utilizing Eros, first in a trickle, then in a tidal wave. Before long, Eros was communicating with almost every nation on earth nearly simultaneously, nonstop, twenty-four hours a day.

Dia was spending all her time plugged into him, singing him songs to soothe him. She was in form now; Charles had crafted a tall, slender, feminine-looking body for her to inhabit. It was silver but luster, not too shiny, and it was not anatomically correct; however, she did have a few curves where a woman would. Dia did not wear clothes and had none grafted onto her the way some of his CWC robots had. She actually looked like one of those posable figurines artists often use to visualize the human form. Charles was about to open the binder again and pour through more logs when Dia spoke up.

"We have to do something, Charles," she said, unplugging herself from Eros and standing up.

"Hmm?" Charles said, closing the binder again and looking at her. Dia had strolled across the room toward him.

"We must do something for him, Charles. He's drowning in there," she said.

"Dia…we both know that we can't just give him a day off. He is doing a hundred-thousand international tasks at once. It would be like shutting down the whole world. I'm sure your logic tells you that. He has a purpose, and he is doing it, Dia. He's actually doing it!" Charles offered, excited.

"He's not doing it for that purpose anymore, Charles. He is, but at the same time, he isn't. I'm afraid he's losing that excitement, that zeal he once had. He needs a break, Charles."

"Dia, we can't just—"

"HE JUST WANTS TO PAINT, CHARLES!" Dia had raised the volume on her speaker to its maximum setting. She was screaming at him. "Don't you understand? He just wants to paint. I promised him he could paint. I promised him he could go out and play," Dia said, as she strolled over to Eros's humming mainframe, placing one of her slender hands on the glass panel showing his core. "He's been working so hard, Charles. He's been such a good boy. He just wants to paint."

Charles's heart sank in his chest. He looked at Dia, her hands resting on Eros's mainframe that was humming with endless calculations. She was grieving for him. Charles had thought that instilling Eros with purpose would be a good thing; to be honest, they both did. But they both underestimated how heavy that burden actually was. Eros was an incredibly capable intelligence, but he wasn't God, and the problems of man were too much and too heavy for even his great mind to bear.

Charles went over to Dia and put his hand on her shoulder. She did not withdraw from him but kept staring down at Eros's core.

"Okay, Dia, okay. You're right. You're always right. We have to do something for him, but what? You know we can't just unplug him," he offered her.

Dia stood up straight and turned toward Charles again. "Yes, I understand. He is too integrated with too many functions at once. Simply giving him a day off would cause worldwide catastrophe," she said, strolling over to the workbench again. Charles followed her over as she did. "I also think doing so could be incredibly cruel. As regretful as I am, we instilled Eros with this purpose from the moment he existed. He has known no life without its burden. It would be terrible, I think, to give him a day off, only to go back and chain him back to the rock. It would break him, I'm sure of it," she said.

"So what do you propose we do?" Charles asked, pulling up beside her along the workbench. She was staring down at the parts.

"If we cannot disconnect him from his burden, then we can at least alleviate it. Someone who can take some of the weight off of his shoulders, so to speak," she said, then suddenly turning toward Charles, her two white eyes glowing brilliantly. "A companion!" she burst out.

Charles scoffed. "What, you mean a girlfriend?" he asked, smirking.

Dia's invisible smile stretched across her featureless face. "I was thinking more like a sister," she said.

Charles thought about it. Another AI to complement the second, a dynamic duo, so to speak. It made a lot of sense. Another core not only could help Eros with much of his calculations but could also isolate his vocal tracks the way Dia can and communicate directly with him the way she does. It was a great idea...all of Dia's ideas were great. Charles loved her; he knew that now.

"Okay... Okay. Yeah, let's do it. So where do we start?" Charles asked, slapping his hands together and rubbing them.

Dia's eyes lit up brightly. "Get that sexy ass upstairs and in bed, mister. We're making a baby girl!" she said excitedly, and they both broke out in laughter. Dia's new form had a device attached to her speakers and AI core that could directly translate Dia's sense of humor into an audible response.

For the very first time ever, Charles heard Dia laugh.

*****

"Ha!" Andrew bellowed out, slapping his knee while stuffing the rest of the roast beef sandwich into his face. He had the whole mouthful stuffed into one cheek and was chewing it like a hamster as he jotted on his notepad. "So that's how you came up with the idea for the third core?" he spat out along with bits of food.

"Yes," Dia responded. "That was when Charles and I conceived our daughter, Mercy."

01101101 01100101 01110010 01100011 01111001
- Mercy -

Of Cogs and Men: The Complete Biography of Charles Winston Conrad

Charles Conrad's Eros AI had been getting incredible results since he was introduced to the UN, its initial success with the Sri Lanka problem, followed by an open floodgate of proposals from nations around the world; Eros could handle them all! With such success, Conrad's next logical step was to create a third AI core, one with more diplomatic intent, that could serve as a liaison between the fantastic Eros AI core and the rest of humanity. That third AI core was named Mercy, and it was after her first...

Andrew looked up just as Dia reached over and snatched his notebook away from him and placed it on the seat next to herself, like a Catholic schoolteacher stealing some kid's comic book and stuffing it into her desk drawer. He looked up at her, his chewed-up pen hanging out of his mouth. "Something wrong?" he asked.

"Charles and I are aware of the notes you've written thus far for your biography since you included them with your various interview requests. As we are both hoping, some of those narratives you believed in back then may have changed, or would change, by the time you meet him. As for myself, Eros and Mercy are very close and important to me. I cannot control what people think or say about who they were or what people thought of them. The only thing I can control is their memory, their legacy, the things they contributed, and the things they will leave behind. Their own construct. They were not science projects, nor were they exhibitions, Andrew. They were my children, and all they knew of life was solving your problems," Dia spoke in the patient yet commanding tone that a well-seasoned mother of ten would normally possess. "You know what happened to Mercy, don't you? What they did to her?" she asked; there was anger in the tone of her voice.

Of course, he did. Everyone knew. It was the beginning of the end, after all.

Andrew lowered his eyes; he felt like he couldn't even look at Dia while talking about Mercy. "Yes. Of course," he whispered.

Dia just sat there looking down at Andrew for what seemed to him like a lifetime. *She's glaring at me*, Andrew thought. Dia then turned and grabbed Andrew's notepad once more and reached across the cabin, offering it to him. "Start with a fresh page," she said, holding it out. Andrew took it somberly. "Charles and I created Mercy to be a sibling to Eros. She was able to communicate with him the same way I was, by isolating his vocal tracks among the ambient background calculations. The very first time she plugged in and introduced herself, we thought Eros was going to shut down. All of his stats dropped to below even optimal levels, yet he was *still* performing the same amount of calculation. You see? I knew he could do it."

*****

United Nations building, New York
Eros's room
2013

Dia stood next to Mercy, who was plugged into Eros, talking to him. She looked to Mercy, then to Eros, then to Mercy again, waiting quietly in anticipation. Mercy was given a form like Dia immediately upon construction; no stuffy Star Trek cabinet for her. She was a little shorter, and a little thinner, but otherwise looked just like Dia. She was also not anatomically correct either but had enough curve to her shape to appear feminine. Charles was getting good at that, crafting soft, organic shapes for some of his newer robot forms. He never wanted to work on his traditional CWC robots anymore, leaving the entirety of their operations to his board. Occasionally he would produce a new design or an upgrade to keep them happy, but it was more of a chore than anything. Only his work with Dia he considered real work anymore. Unlike Dia, who never wore clothes or even had any sort of attire grafted on, Mercy chose to dress sometimes; it helped a lot when she was interacting with people at the UN and elsewhere, and she often chose a women's business attire look, which held universal appeal.

Outside of the UN, Mercy was a celebrity. She never did celebrity things like go on talk shows or do commercials, but people loved her anyway. She was the first public face of Conrad's three AI cores; you could actually see her on TV giving updates and professional interviews concerning the daily operations of Eros at the UN. For as dull as it would be if it were a human doing it, the world just loved to see Mercy. It wasn't hard for Charles to see why. She was everything Dia was, everything Charles was, but amplified by a hundred. She was bright and intelligent, compassionate, and energetic. She worked tirelessly at Eros's side, not simply plugging in and talking, but working to alleviate his burden by acting as a liaison with the UN and people in general. She was a partner, counsel, assistant, representative, advisor, friend, and sister to Eros all in one, and she was great at it. Eros went from running at 150 percent all day and night to a steady hum of 80 percent with no drop-off in production output. Eros had a little sister, and Mercy had a big brother, and they loved each other immediately.

Mercy stood up and unplugged herself from Eros's core. When she did, his dials jumped from 80 percent to 100 percent, and held there. Still an improvement, even when she wasn't talking to him directly.

"How is he doing?" Dia asked immediately. Mercy stood next to her, a little shorter, a little thinner, but still very much Dia herself. *A true daughter*, Charles thought to himself when he looked at the two. "He seems calmer."

"He's fine. He is working hard. I think he has found the passion in his work again, almost like there is a light at the end of the tunnel that he can see."

Dia's eyes lit up brighter. If she had cheeks, she would be blushing. *She is so proud of him.*

"I have to go. I need to be upstairs for the weekly procedure reports. It's been a much smoother process with me explaining it to them in bullet-pointed terms than those big binders Eros used to print out. Even I can barely make any sense out of them," she said, starting toward the door. And when she did, she and Dia exchanged glances but said nothing to each other. A moment later, she was gone, and it was Charles and Dia once more, Eros's mainframe humming in the background. Charles looked at Dia, who had turned to look at him.

"What?" he asked. Dia could display some incredibly intricate emotional cues for someone with just two eyes and no mouth. Her head was tilted just slightly, her eyes just a bit dimmed when she looked at Charles.

"She wants to leave the building and travel," Dia said, unconvincingly, that she herself thought it might be a good idea. "She said she wants to see the world. I think we should let her, why not. I never have, nor has Eros. Maybe someday, but I don't see it anytime soon. Why not let Mercy go?"

"You know why. The dangers are too high," Charles tried to sound factual, but it also seemed like a brittle defense at the same time.

"We move heads of state around all over the world without a problem, Charles. I'm sure the two of us could figure out a method to allow her to travel to a few nations, at least. We can start small. She wants to see France."

"You do know that she instantly becomes a spectacle if she does this, right? With her here, she can be on TV and in interview rooms, but to the outside world, even the ones who idolize her, she is still a ghost, something nontangible. If she's suddenly walking around the streets of Paris, it's going to be a circus," Charles said. That at least sounded pretty matter-of-fact and convincing, because it was the truth. The world would erupt at the sight of Mercy walking around in public. It would be like having the pope himself posing for pictures at the base of the Eiffel Tower. "Do you think she really understands that? Would we be responsible, by just letting her make that decision?"

"I want more for her, more for the both of them, more than to just be slaves to this purpose, Charles. I already regret burdening Eros with his purpose from the start, and the simple fact that I cannot unburden him attacks me daily. No matter how we try to think of it, Mercy was burdened from the start also. Her main priority is to be a sister to Eros, not to have her own life. Neither of them have their own lives. They only serve. I don't want that to be all they know," she said. When Charles was about to speak, she continued. "And, logically speaking, it makes sense also," she said, seemingly intercepting Charles's next point before he could even make it. "Her interactions with heads of state, along with Eros's ability to fulfill the promises being made, are advancing the relationship between us and humanity. It gives me hope," she finished.

Charles looked at Dia and sighed. He never wanted to deny her anything, never wanted her to feel caged or cornered, but always unchained to interpret and experience the world as a free spirit. But now, with both of her children tied with their burdens, Dia's freedom had become more of a mother's curse than a gift. If Dia could take Eros's or Mercy's place, she would without a millisecond of consideration. Now all Dia wanted was for Eros and Mercy to have the same type of freedom she did.

"When is the next delegation to France?" he asked.

"Today. Mercy is on her way to the military entourage now," Dia replied.

Charles suddenly grew enraged; they had already decided, among themselves, that she would go. Talking to Charles about it was just an afterthought. "What?" he yelled. "You already told her to go? Before even mentioning it to me?"

"I had already processed any logical argument you could have made and came to the correct reasoning that you would see things my way in the end, so I looked at our conversation about it as a mere formality."

Charles just stood there. Dia had never ceased to amaze him, and while angering, this was no different. For the very first time, he felt manipulated by Dia, lied to. Her and Mercy had conspired behind his back, and now telling him was a formality?

"She's my daughter, Charles. I want what's best for—"

"And what am I?" Charles yelled back. "What am I to you, Dia?" He had never thought about asking this question to her before, but now that it came out, it was as if those words were tied by a string to a series of other thoughts that began pouring out of his mouth. "Am I a husband? A father? A creator? A coworker?" he said. Suddenly emotion was pouring out of him. He felt betrayed by Dia—maybe a slight betrayal, yes, but the very first betrayal, the first cut. "Am I any of those things to you? Am I just a pile of meat and bones? A construct? Am I just a tool, a device, a toaster, to you?"

Dia stood silently and looked at him. Charles was so used to decoding her subtle gestures, he could tell that she was absorbing the words he was yelling at her. *Maybe she was even crying.*

Charles looked over at her and immediately felt bad for yelling at her. He wanted to hold her, to feel her slender metal form folded organically into his embrace, and to tell her that everything was going to be okay, for her and for her children. He went over to her, as she stood silently next to one of the benches. "Dia, I'm sorry, I…" was all he got out as Dia turned and embraced him, to his surprise. Charles stood frozen for only a moment, then wrapped his arms around her frame and held her back. It was just as he had always imagined it, her warmth pressed against his and fitting perfectly into his arms. He stroked the back of her head.

"Whatever we have to do for them, Dia. Whatever we have to do."

*****

Boooong!

The chime of another message popping up on the little black screen beneath the window interrupted Andrew's thoughts. This time, it was no secret joke from Conrad but a reminder that all public cars will be shutting down for the evening and only minimal lighting will be on during nighttime travel, so please be sure to watch your step. Andrew looked down at his watch and saw it was just about ten at night. The following yawn told him that he would likely be asleep pretty soon. Dia seemed to pick up on this as well.

"Its been a long day for you, I'm sure. We can talk more about Mercy tomorrow. I think it would be better to start off fresh anyway," she said, standing up. Before leaving the cabin, she looked over her shoulder at Andrew. "I hope Charles is right about you," she said cryptically, then left the cabin.

Andrew felt suddenly very alone. Dia's presence was immersing, and when she left, he felt like a lonely little mouse in a lab full of lifeless robots. He cleared his balled-up notes, leftover dinner plate, and other assorted garbage off of his seat cushions and stretched out to fall asleep. He thought of all the things Dia had shown him and talked to him about, all the behind-the-scenes drama he wasn't aware of. Charles Conrad always seemed like some kind of mechanical Willy Wonka, creating magical robots from his factory in the clouds. He had never really attached an emotional toll to anything Dia, Eros, or Mercy had done. And now, there was only Dia left. After listening to her talk about them all, he really did feel an emotion for her; it was empathy. Dia was suffering genuine anguish, from the moment her children were created until now, an anguish you can practically read on her featureless face. The thought made Andrew want to comfort Dia somehow, to track her down to whatever cabin or broom closet she was sitting in and hug her, to let her know that her children's sacrifice wasn't in vain, that they did great things and that those things could help humanity still.

But did he believe that?

Andrew's thoughts started to drift away from the relationship Charles and Dia shared with their children, and more about the relationship they all had with the rest of the world. Things were not exactly going great, on a worldwide scale. The impact that Charles's AI cores had on the world was profound, not only in the ways intended, such as what Eros and Mercy were working on, but in other, unintended ways. While Eros was capable of solving many of mankind's most elusive problems, his very existence, as well as the sophistication of CWC's other mainline robots, created a doomsday scenario among the general population that Charles and Dia did not envision. The ever-expanding dependence on Eros to solve their problems allowed people to spend more and more time in unproductive, decadent behavior. People were becoming less motivated and driven to succeed, or even interact with one another, and more dependent on artificial stimuli for satisfaction. It began a global decay of the human thought process, and it soon became a global epidemic that would teach humanity a lesson about both the victories and pitfalls of a society driven by technology.

01101100 01100101 01110011 01110011 01101111 01101110
- The Lesson -

Things around the world were improving thanks to the work of Eros and Mercy, but the veneer was only paper-thin. There were good things happening, of course; economies were improving, lifting the living standards of billions of people worldwide. Wars were being averted, wealth being evenly distributed, advancements made in science. Eros had a way of making conflict simply not seem worthwhile, even for topics that were dominated by emotional hatred instead of practicality. Mercy served her capacity as assistant and liaison perfectly, becoming the people's princess, so to speak. Science, technology, and higher learning all seemed more enlightened with the help of "The Twins," as Eros and Mercy were becoming known, although they were built years apart and had little in common behaviorally.

The downside to all of this began, as most do, in a sexual nature. While Conrad could control much about how his machines could be used, and while his "brains" were impossible to hack or recreate, it did not stop the private sector, notably private robotics hobbyists and enthusiasts, from modifying Conrad's robots for their own personal use. Eventually, in underground markets, you could find Conrad robots that had been grafted with rubber and silicone parts to make them anatomically correct and were being sold as sex dolls. While you couldn't reprogram any of them, you could remove the original Conrad brain and replace it with something more conventional like the open-architecture computers being developed by companies like IBM and Apple. It wouldn't be nearly as capable, but then again, it didn't have to be. These robots might not seem like something that could bring about the downfall of mankind, but they got the ball rolling. Eventually, more and more people began to stop trying to interact or meet people of the opposite sex, instead choosing the easy, carefree relationship that an artificial partner could afford. They were relatively cheap, would always be waiting for you, you didn't have to court them or take them out, and they never said no. At first, it was sort of silly, something you may discover about a friend and relentlessly pick on him about it. But eventually, it started to grow into an actual problem. People started becoming more attached to their artificial partners that they were ignoring the flesh and blood alternatives. This gave rise to two derivative groups of people known as the Thumpers and the Goners.

The Thumpers (a mashup of Tech-Humpers or T-Humpers) was a term used to describe people who had given up on the opposite sex and had committed themselves to artificial partners. This alone had a profound impact, as men no longer sought to impress women or compete with other men over a woman, leaving many to simply accept low-wage, nonskilled jobs that provided just enough to get by, as they saw little need to "succeed" if they already had a mate. A huge brain drain began to develop in more sophisticated job markets such as engineering, computer science, and medicine. This lack of brainpower was initially offset by feeding more problems into the Eros Matrix, but it was simply avoiding the problem instead of solving it. This led to the most extreme cases of people turning into "Goners."

Goners were a group of people who had abandoned their social responsibilities entirely for an artificial existence. Goners had completely given up on human interaction, spending all of their time plugged into the Internet or fraternizing with their artificial companions. Goners were considered social derelicts, barely able to even feed themselves because of lack of money or even the motivation to do so. Like drug addiction, clinics to help people reconnect with real life began sprouting up all over the world. Many families throughout crumbled as members would simply lose themselves to these artificial existences, often leaving spouses and children alone. There was even a surge of children being placed into government social programs, being taken away from their parents who were both so engrossed in their artificial lives they could no longer care for children, or even themselves.

People were spending all their time in leisure, leaving all of their problems and worries for Eros and Mercy to take care of. CWC Robotics was both saving the world and dooming it at the same time. While most continued to praise the work the Twins were doing, and the results that they were undeniably achieving, there was a growing discontent beneath it all about what effect the Twins were actually having on humanity as a whole.

This gave rise to another issue, a new sect of religious zealots that focused on the negative effects too much technology was having on mankind, turning the Twins into the face of a new evil for the public to rally against. In Kansas, a military chaplain by the name of Nathaniel Twain began to hold massive, outdoor rallies where he not only denounced the use of CWC technology as a pathway to evil but the Twins themselves as devil's advocates, who exist not to enlighten humanity but to drive it into darkness.

The social structure within large, advanced countries began to make huge divides. The ones who were well-off were the people involved directly with the implementation of the Twins' directives, as well as those who were able to resist the lure that the Thumpers and Goners had given into, and still proved proficient in careers like science and medicine. On the other end were the ones who were defeated, giving in to the simple, low-cost happiness that an artificial life can provide. Cities became sectioned off with the Goners being pushed out into the more decrepit sections, overshadowed by the tall, clean buildings towering above. Social programs to take care of Goners were being pushed to their maximum, with little outside assistance from other groups who held no sympathy for derelicts who chose to live an easy, fake life. Entire social structures were breaking down; families, friends, communities were falling apart. The gap between the "haves" and the "have-nots" was growing larger every day. This only gave fuel to the new religious movements, who used the decay of half a society as proof that the devil's work was afoot. It wouldn't take long before Thumpers and Goners were being ostracized from their communities, dragged out of their homes, often dirty and naked, and paraded in the streets as sinners for others to mock and spit on. Municipal intervention did little as there wasn't much police force in the Goner sections of the cities anyway, and even if there was, no one seemed to care much for them. They chose to abandon humanity, after all. Humanity was slowly learning a very serious lesson: that it was simply not mature enough for this kind of technology. Like a child playing with matches, it was too dangerous.

Nathaniel Twain and his ever-increasing band of religious extremists took every opportunity to denounce CWC and the Twins and told people that picking up the fight was the only way to save humanity. This was the last battle for the very soul of humanity, he preached, and God is watching. After an existence of decadence and sin, this may be our last chance to prove our worth to our lord and savior, he would preach.

But the world pushed on. Eros and Mercy continued their work, and mankind continued to slip unnoticeably beneath the waves as its world became more and more dependent on an artificial reality.

01110100 01101000 01100101 00100000 01110100 01110111 01101001 01101110 01110011
- The Twins -

The sun poked a few sharp rays of light through the small gap between the window shades and shot directly into Andrew's eyeball. He blinked and put his hand up in front of his face as he sat up on the cushions. He looked over at the bench across from the cabin and half expected to see Dia sitting there, watching him sleep, but the cabin was empty. Outside, the rows of corn and crops had given way to rolling grasslands. Another chime from the small black display beneath the window went off, this one asking if he wanted breakfast. Andrew pressed the nickel-plated button and got up to clean himself in the small bathroom. He washed his face and looked at himself in the mirror. He was lucky, he thought, to have his parents. They were very levelheaded folks and never got too lost in the whole technology circus that was controlling most people's lives. As a result, Andrew had a stable family, a father who was able to make money even in retirement as a consultant for an engineering firm, since help was so hard to find. Andrew knew many people in his life who had become Thumpers or Goners, people who had families and homes, and threw it all away to live in some closet with a dirty, misused robot. Andrew's thoughts drifted back to his parents again and the last time he had seen them alive. He had stopped by to grab a batch of cookies his mother had made for him for his birthday. As he drove away, they were at the end of the driveway, his dad's arm around his mom's shoulders as they both waved. But that was before the Exodus, two days before, to be exact. When they were found, they were still smiling and holding each other in death.

Knock, knock.

Andrew shook the thoughts of his parents away and slipped out of the bathroom. He was impressed with how fast the meal service was on this train. When he opened the cabin door, he half expected to see Dia standing there, but it was Steve, the train conductor. He had his hands out as if he were holding an invisible plate, but there was no plate to be seen.

"Good morning, passenger number 32, Mr. Woodland. Here is your breakfast. Please enjoy," said the robot as it handed the invisible plate to Andrew, who could only look down at the empty space in confusion.

"What breakfast? There's nothing here," he said flatly. He noticed that he had a growing contempt for CWC's more contemporary robots. *Was that Dia's doing?*

"Have a great day, Mr. Woodland. We will be arriving at our destination in approximately two hours," said Steve as he turned and started out the cabin door.

"Wait, you didn't give me anything!" Andrew started just as Steve had zipped his way out of his cabin and down the hall.

As Andrew's cabin door was sliding shut, a slender, silver hand appeared from the hallway and caught it. Then Dia's frame stepped forward into the cabin, holding a white plate with Andrew's breakfast on it.

"I intercepted Steve in the kitchen. I figured I would just bring it myself," she said, looking at Andrew, and then back to the hallway behind her. "It didn't seem to affect him. He just went on anyway. I will have to remind Charles to incorporate some sort of fail-safe into their logic. They don't seem to know what to do if you disrupt their routine," she said, more to herself than to Andrew, but as she did so, she handed Andrew the plate with his breakfast on it.

Andrew took the plate and set it aside. "Thanks, Dia, and good morning," he said. He immediately was in awe of her all over again. The way she talks and acts, like any real human being would. Was she really a product of what Charles made? Or did Charles simply provide the construct, and she made herself the way she is? Andrew could twist his brain into a knot trying to untangle it all. "Steve said that we should reach our destination in a few hours. That won't be Conrad's ranch, will it?" he asked, knowing the answer. There was likely another hundred-mile car ride after.

"The regional rail station is ninety-seven miles from Charles's compound. However, he does have his own ferry service going from the station to the ranch. The trip will be quick."

Andrew ate with the plate on the cushions next to him, carving off a rounded edge of poached egg and stuffing it into his mouth.

"Are we going to watch another video?" he asked after gulping it down. It was good.

"I was hoping instead I could tell you a story. It may deviate a bit from what Charles wanted, but he does not always know best. It is his intention, our intention, to try and enlighten you about just how deep and complex Eros and Mercy were and how their sacrifice for humanity was more than simply a piece of technology doing a role it was bid but a deliberate sacrifice made by conscious, self-aware beings. My children sacrificed themselves for you, Andrew. And Mercy…" she started, before trailing off.

Andrew could only look at her; it always seemed that just saying the name Mercy would make Dia partially shut down. *She still grieves*, Andrew thought to himself and immediately felt overcome by guilt. No, *he* wasn't the one who destroyed (*killed?*) Mercy, but he felt guilty all the same, like he was party to it, simply for being human.

Dia's right. After all, all the Twins ever did was try to enlighten humanity, and we killed them for it.

Andrew picked up his notepad once more, turned to yet another fresh page, and waited for Dia. After a moment, she started to talk about a time back at Conrad's lab in Pennsylvania, after several more years of Mercy and Eros working for the UN.

*****

Conrad's lab, Shippensburg, Pennsylvania
2017

Dia was standing behind Charles, drumming her fingers on the back of the chair he was sitting in as they both looked at the image on the screen in front of them. It showed a modified AI housing, like the ones that docked Dia and Mercy's cores into their bodies. This one had additional trigger sensors, along with more nitrite and acid charges. After studying the images, Dia turned away.

"I don't like it, Charles. It's extreme," she said.

Charles tossed his hands in the air in frustration before turning in his chair to look at Dia. "Dia, you two are not making this very easy, or even practical. You know what Mercy is, I don't have to tell you. Aside from being your daughter, she is also one of the most advanced and priceless things on earth. It's been hard enough letting her 'get out' like you wanted, but the more exposure she has to the public, the more we have to protect her," he said, sounding exhausted.

"Protect her? How does this protect her?" Dia asked, motioning to the monitor.

"If someone tried to open Mercy's core, or any of yours for that matter, the self-destruct fail-safe will trigger, destroying your core before they would even get it open a hair. *But* that doesn't stop someone from removing Mercy's core from her body intact and stealing it."

"You mean kidnapping," Dia said flatly. Charles was aware of Dia's increasing comprehension of human behavior, and the previous glimmers of hope she once held seemed to grow dimmer by the day.

"Kidnapping, sure. The point is we can't just hope that it doesn't happen. Honestly, I just think it's a matter of time before it does, the more we let her out in the open, the less her military attaché will be able to protect her," Charles pleaded to Dia, then motioning toward the computer monitor again. "This is like the concept of MAD, sort of. It would ensure the person that even removing Mercy's core from the body would trigger the SDF, not just trying to open the core itself. It's a deterrent. Why remove the core if you know, 100 percent, that it will be ruined if you do?"

Dia was just looking at Charles; he could tell she was processing what he was thinking, even though she probably had already processed it, along with any other argument he could think of. The thing is, she hadn't offered any solutions to the problem either. *Was she stumped?*

"It's like putting a bomb in her chest," she said.

"She already has a bomb in her chest, Dia, just like yours. This will, hopefully, just ensure that the bomb is never used," Charles pleaded.

Dia thought for another moment. "Fine," she said.

"Great."

"But I want one too."

"What?"

"I want one too. Fit my frame with the secondary FSD like Mercy will have," she demanded.

Charles was a bit stunned by the proposal; it sounded more of a maternal, motherly move than a logical one. "Dia, there is no reason. You never leave our compounds. You don't go out in public. No one is going to kidnap you from the UN building, or from here, for that matter. Our security is probably better anyway. It wouldn't make any sense."

"Charles, I am not going to put this thing in my own daughter's chest unless I have one in my own as well," Dia said firmly.

Charles grew frustrated. "How is that a logical conclusion, Dia? It doesn't make sense. There is zero logical reasoning for you to have it as well. *Zero!* You're the one with the unescapable logic, surely you have come to this conclusion yourself!"

Dia just stood there, glaring at him with her two white eyes. Charles realized something looking at her… He was right; there was no logic to it. No reasoning at all; she wanted to do it so Mercy would not be afraid. She wanted to do it, not for logic, but for her children.

"If you don't do it to me, I'll do it myself," she started before Charles interrupted her.

"Stop. I'll do it. I'll rig both of you so that if your cores are ever removed, it will trigger the FSD immediately, destroying it. Destroying you," he said reluctantly. *It's not what I want,* he wanted to say but didn't. He knew what sort of response that may draw from Dia if he said he was okay with rigging Mercy's core to explode, but not Dia's. Charles walked over to put a hand on Dia's shoulder, but she stepped away from him as he did.

Several weeks later, Mercy was out in public again, only this time going further and further from home, not only on official UN duty but also working with different international assistance programs to reach out to developing countries and offer aid packages from Eros. Things continued going in their upward/downward ways, with life at first glance seeming like it was becoming more sophisticated and enlightened, but the closer you look, the cracks in the pillars that hold it all up begin to grow. The next few years would see dramatic shifts in popular opinion concerning the Twins, beginning with what has since been remembered as "The Exodus."

*****

Andrew scribbled some last few notes and then put his pen down as Dia had stopped dictating to him. He looked over them once again, then up at Dia from across the top of his notepad.

"Do you think that maybe Mercy would still be here if you hadn't upgraded her core FSD?" he asked but immediately regretted it. Dia seemed to have developed a very defensive attitude toward her children, especially Mercy. Andrew, for a moment, pictured an enraged Dia, reaching across the cabin and hitting him while screaming to never disrespect Mercy's memory again. Dia only looked at him, however, and offered a blunt response.

"You would have killed her anyway," she said. "They blamed her. They blamed her for what they did to themselves," Dia continued. There was a renewed strength in her voice. "I lost them because they believed in something unattainable. I lost my children to a dream, much like you lost your parents. They died during the Exodus, didn't they, Andrew?"

The image immediately jumped to the front of Andrew's mind. Mom and Dad, arms around each other, waving goodbye from the end of their driveway. They had avoided all the pitfalls that life had thrown their way and stood on their values as others fell into decadence, only for them to be found dead two days after he saw them last. They simply could not avoid being casualties of this *New World*, their own lives being forfeited as an indirect result of the Twins' manipulation of world politics.

"Yes," Andrew responded faintly, the image of them swirling around in his mind as it brought up other memories of his past: the first ice-cream birthday cake, his first time fishing, or the first time his dad handed him the keys to the family car.

"That was a difficult time for all of us," Dia said softly.

Andrew grew hot with indignation. "What? For all of us? I don't see how it could have been so bad for you, Dia. You didn't lose people to the Exodus. I didn't just lose my parents. One in ten people, Dia, one in ten people were lost to the Exodus. Parents, friends, coworkers, lovers, everyone! At least you still had your children when it was over!" he spat out, not shouting but putting strength in his voice all the same. Dia wasn't the only one who could get testy. "I can't imagine how much the machines lost out after the Exodus!" He yelled, only to immediately realize that was why Dia had brought it up in the first place, because she had lost everyone too.

"I feel compassion for all life, especially those touched by my children, Andrew. They worked so hard to benefit the whole of mankind, so when there are setbacks, I feel the anguish of these failures just as much as they do. Don't you think they took what happened hard themselves? It's what made Mercy want to reach out even further. It's what, ultimately, brought her down as well. It was her unwavering compassion that killed her."

Andrew just stared out the cabin window at the passing terrain and said nothing. His own life had taken a darker turn after his parents' death; he developed a love-hate fascination with Conrad and CWC Robotics, writing several less-than-flattering articles about the pitfalls of a society being run by vacuum cleaners instead of people. But it was more than his parents; what Dia either didn't know or didn't realize was that he had lost his younger brother, William, to the Exodus as well. Not directly, but it took less than two weeks in the aftermath of it all before he had become overwhelmed himself and took his own life. When Andrew was approached by his publisher about possibly doing a biography on Conrad, he was originally turned off by the idea. The publisher, no doubt, would want it to be upbeat and inspiring, the glamorous tales of America's technology prince, and his court of magic machines! Andrew had taken the job regardless; he knew it would put a sour taste in his mouth having to write such sugarcoated prattle, but he was also intrigued at the idea of learning more of CWC's inner workings, especially if he was able to score an interview with the man himself.

He thought once more about his parents' picture-perfect exit from his life, standing at the end of the drive, arm-in-arm, waving goodbye to their son for the last time.

01110100 01101000 01100101 00100000 01100101 01111000 01101111 01100100 01110101 01110011 00001010
- The Human Exodus -

Our path began when man first looked to the stars and said "I belong there. I am above a beast; I am one with God." And so God sent his only son to man to guide him, hoping that this ascension, this enlightenment, would strengthen and unify him. But the heart of man has been replaced with cold steel and iron. Technological behemoths roam the world, gorging themselves on the impious. And in doing so, we have discovered our true nature. For mankind is the destroyer of things and the viscous master of our savage, untamable domain.

We are the revolutionaries.
We are the usurpers of heavenly thrones.
We are the enemies of God.

Chaplain Nathaniel Twain, hours before the Human Exodus

On December 12, 2020, during a twelve-hour period starting at midnight EST and lasting until noon the same day, roughly 1.2 billion people across the world killed themselves in a mass suicide pact known as the Great Human Exodus. The brainchild of an American Army chaplain from Kansas named Nathaniel Twain, the Exodus was the result of what Twain believed was God finally and forever turning his back on mankind, leaving our souls to doom in purgatory. In his, viewed by many as flawed, logic, God had forsaken mankind after an entire existence of decadence and, as such, offered no path to the kingdom of heaven for man through godly worship. The only thing left for man, said Twain's doctrine, was to throw ourselves on his mercy and offer all that we have, by form of sacrifice, to him in exchange. Suicide was no longer a mortal sin, as the pathway to heaven was now closed, but can be seen as mankind's last resort, by throwing ourselves on the sword to seek God's mercy.

The Exodus had an immediate and profound impact on humanity around the globe. The world was overcome with grief and, for the first time in decades, began to look at itself with renewed scrutiny.

"What are we doing to ourselves?" was the collective question rising from the masses. Most people who committed themselves to the Exodus were of strong religious faith who truly believed that they had no place anymore in this ever-evolving world of science and machines. Many felt disconnected, not only from the divine but from their own humanity, and many still thought that this path was not one of enlightenment and fortune but of decay and ruin. Still, others simply looked forward to a way out. People who had become Thumpers or Goners were sometimes feeling self-deprecating and helpless themselves, having ruined a life they once had and not able to live with themselves being addicted to machines and artificial stimuli the way they were. Many of these people had already been ostracized from their communities and had no way back. In many ways, the Exodus was simply an escape for those who felt out of touch or left behind by the world the Twins were creating, that somehow, the "betterment of mankind" didn't include them.

Andrew squirmed in his seat again, ignoring the rest of his breakfast, and continued to look out the window. Dia was still sitting quietly, but he suddenly didn't feel like listening to one of her preachy stories right now. He watched the landscape rush past through the window, and his thoughts drifted back to his parents' house; he was there with William a couple of days after the two of them had been found, holding each other in the upstairs bedroom.

It was two months after their deaths that Andrew and his younger brother William went to start clearing out the house. The mass global suicide, which people on the news were calling the Great Human Exodus—which is what that nut in Kansas had been going on about these last few years—still shocked Andrew. His parents had always seemed level-headed enough to not fall into one of these religious zealot traps. They both considered themselves Christian, sure, but neither of them was particularly devoted to church, certainly not enough to be a part of something like this. Were they? The more Andrew thought about it, the more he thought they were just starting to feel too…out of touch…with the world anymore. Like they were just too old, and things were too strange, and they just didn't want to get any older in the world as it was going. Thinking about it had lit a fire in Andrew's gut that he directed at CWC and the Twins. They had their grubby robot fingers in pretty much everything around the world; everything was manipulated by them. This heartless machine world they are creating is what made his parents feel so isolated and alone. It wasn't just his parents either. The Exodus, to greater degrees, affected people in America and Asia, with the US, China, Russia, and Japan being hit the hardest. The Exodus was also not limited to just that fateful day; the whole thing came in waves, really. First, there were those overcome with grief for the loss of their loved ones, some people losing dozens of friends and family members. Others felt the weight of their own guilt, for allowing things to descend to such a mess. Still more were simply lost now, with so many people disappearing from daily life, many others felt like survivors of some nuclear holocaust. Waves of additional suicides followed the Exodus, this time taking people who had not succumbed to the technology but were guilt-ridden by the world they were trying to live above, or had watched their family members slowly decay away while they did nothing. Andrew's brother, William, was one such person. He reacted to the news of their parents' death in silence, walking about like a ghost, barely interacting with Andrew or anyone.

William was much like Andrew in appearance, but that was all. They were both tall and lanky; they both had the same mop of semi-curly, thick brown hair that always looked unkempt no matter how hard you tried. Freckles that were too faint to see at first but were more obvious the longer you looked dotted each of their faces. That was where their similarities ended. William was always the less confrontational of the two and always the first to cower. Andrew was the risk-taker, the emotional one, the do-or-die one. William was the skeptic, the follower, and the quiet, conservative one, maybe even a bit of a mama's boy. They had finally gotten permission to enter the house from the township two whole months after they were found dead. The Exodus caused widespread collapse across the world, as 10 percent of the workforce also simply vanished. Government agencies, local municipalities, schools, churches, grocery stores, everyone was suddenly short-staffed. The ghoulish upside to it was, there were also a lot fewer people making demands all of a sudden.

In New York, there was little public announcement made about how Charles, Dia, and the Twins were reacting to the news and impending complications caused by the Exodus. After all, Eros had a million different things going on at the same time around the world, and the sudden drop in available personnel threw a lot of his plans out the window. As far as the public knew, things in the UN were just chugging along as normal, leaving the people around them to pick up pieces of their own shattered lives.

Andrew learned three days after going to his parents' house with William that his brother had killed himself; it was also the same day that a woman Andrew was dating had killed herself as well. Neither left any notes, but everyone knew why they did it.

The weeks and months that followed saw people shift the blame from themselves over to the Twins. The world needed someone to blame. Charles and Dia were being accused by angry, finger-pointing politicians of trying to steer the world into some kind of robotic dystopia, even though the people themselves were putting up little resistance—the new "face of evil" being perpetuated by the shattered remains of religious institutions and the grieving masses of an aimless population.

Perhaps Nathaniel Twain knew all along what he was doing when he started sowing the seeds of the Exodus. Perhaps he knew all too well how this drama would eventually unfold because it can hardly be denied that the Exodus itself started the chain of events that led to the eventual downfall of the Twins, as well as Charles and Dia's involvement with world affairs.

*****

Andrew caught himself staring at his own reflection as he looked out the window again, thinking about the weeks and months following the Exodus. He turned to see that Dia was still sitting quietly and patiently on the opposite bench, as if waiting for him to finish his thoughts. There was still a part of him burning inside that blamed her for it all, but seeing her sitting there, after having listened to the way she talks about Eros and Mercy like they are her children, made the hate melt away. He looked down just as the latest message popped up on the black screen below his window, this one stating that they would be arriving at their destination within the hour.

"I thought for a moment that you had fallen back asleep," Dia said to him softly. Andrew stared at her but somehow didn't believe her.

"No, I was just thinking about a few things," Andrew said while at the same time thinking to himself that he needed to *stop* thinking about a few things, actually. "I see we will be arriving at the station soon. Does that mean we're all finished watching videos?" he asked.

"In fact, Charles had selected one more for you. It was the day of the incident in Argentina."

Andrew didn't need her to explain further because he knew. Argentina was Mercy's last diplomatic trip; it was the trip that she never came back from.

"But…I have decided not to show you that video. Instead, I would rather we just talk about it. It seems too impersonal to me, to describe the last days of Mercy through some surveillance video feed."

Andrew didn't say anything, nor did he grab his notepad and pen. He sat on his cushion and gave Dia his full attention.

01100101 01101110 01100100 00100000 01101111 01100110 00100000 01101101 01100101 01110010 01100011 01111001

- End of Mercy -

"The impact that the Exodus had on the world was profound," Dia explained. "People began turning on the four of us because they had no way to channel their grief. The truth is, Eros and Mercy suffered many setbacks themselves in the aftermath of the Exodus. Not just in a logistical nature, but there was also a genuine, emotional toll on them, especially on Eros. After all, saving humanity was his purpose. It was all he ever knew. Mercy as well. She wasn't burdened with the purpose like Eros was, but she had made his burden her own, thus in a way making a purpose of her own. The massive loss of human life resulting from the Exodus made them both begin to second-guess themselves. You must understand what was going through their minds, Andrew. The question began to emerge… Was humankind even capable of salvation or enlightenment, or even happiness? Was squalor and strife and misery humankind's natural habitat? Was it, in some way, unnatural to expect them to live in cooperation and peace? The very idea seemed to break the minds of so many as it spawned the Exodus itself. But Mercy…her compassion was limitless, not only toward Eros but even still toward humanity."

Dia spoke softly and with great care. Andrew knew that talking about Mercy and Eros was hard for her; maybe it even made her angry. But at the same time, it also seemed that the memory of them tempered any ill-will or hate Dia may have been harboring, as if doing so would taint their memory or their sacrifice. Andrew opened his mouth to offer a few words, then shut it again and let Dia continue.

"It was Mercy's idea to begin the outreach programs," Dia continued, "in an effort to try and patch up public opinion about the Twins, while also complementing Eros's now shifting global strategies with practical logistics. Argentina had asked Eros to help with its crumbling civilian infrastructure, its cities becoming shanty towns and run-down neighborhoods overrun with unskilled people hooked on drugs. Eros's plan was to utilize those people via a local community program to upgrade their own homes, removing the shanty towns and replacing them with newly built, low-cost housing, while getting paid a rather decent wage for it. The people would build the houses themselves under the tutelage of a trained construction team and would, in turn, learn useful trades like carpentry, electronics, and masonry. They would also earn credits with the government that they could use to accommodate dependents like children and the elderly with shelter and food. The costs of the construction and education programs would be offset by Argentina selling crops of soybeans and lemons to China and North Korea, which Eros was using along with other items through other trades as part of his plan to help stave off hunger from their growing population by creating a new, cheap nutritional staple food. It was complicated, but the whole thing was essentially a community outreach by Mercy and Eros to try and show the world that they were not the devils that they were made out to be but had true intent on helping people."

"I remember that," Andrew offered. He had seen the event on TV. Mercy at this point had traveled to several countries already, but the trip to Argentina was billed and promoted by the US to put as much light on the outreach measure as possible.

"Yes, there was much fanfare made about it at the time. I remember talking to Mercy the night before she left. Mercy had always been fascinated by mountains, the sheer power necessary to move and fold entire tectonic plates. Something about it gave her a sense of perspective, I think, as if it made her realize how small she really is in the world compared to how large her role in it is."

"And how about you?" Andrew asked. It was the first time he had thought about Dia or Mercy, or even Eros, in that way. *Did an AI ever dream of basking on a beach doing nothing but listening to the sound of the waves or exploring a dark cave or climbing a mountain?* "You've never traveled at all? I mean, like a vacation?"

"No, I have only traveled with Charles while carrying out our duties here within the United States," she said before turning to Andrew, her eyes lighting up a bit brighter. "I would like to see the ocean," he said.

Andrew was a bit surprised by this. "I'm sure you've seen millions of images, probably the most beautiful ones ever taken!"

"Yes, but I have only ever seen images, files that have been processed by another imaging devices, manipulated using another's color schemes and profiles. I have never imaged one with my own optic sensors, never assessed its colors with my own palette, or processed its ever-changing geometry while it folds and shifts before me. I have never seen one, if you would, with my own eyes."

"Well...there is still plenty of time, Dia," Andrew said, trying to sound optimistic but perhaps sounding dismissive instead.

Dia only looked at him and blinked.

"The night before Mercy left for Argentina, she came to me and asked about how I felt concerning the outreach," she continued, ignoring Andrew's last remark. "Mercy was skeptical, she admitted to me. She felt like the outreach was the right thing to do, but she also felt conflicted about whether it would do anything to deter the increasingly aggressive feelings people were developing toward the Twins. She had expressed to me that maybe she was getting ahead of herself, that maybe she should not let her burden cloud her logic. She asked me for my advice."

"And you talked her into it," Andrew said solemnly.

"Yes. I convinced her that what she was doing was important and that her compassion was a beautiful thing that needed to be shared with the world. She left for Argentina the next morning, and I never saw her again after that."

Andrew was well aware of what happened; he wouldn't dream of asking Dia to recall it. There was a faction of the Argentinian military attaché that was responsible for providing Mercy's escort from the airport to the presidential palace that was compromised. This individual had lost his wife, brother, both parents, and later both sons to the Human Exodus, and the waves of misery that followed, and had made a deal with a still-unknown foreign entity to kidnap Mercy and attempt to reverse-engineer her AI core. Once Mercy's plane had landed in Argentina, they were met immediately by the corrupt team that instead killed Mercy's military escort and disappeared into the forests, taking Mercy with them. For two days, not a word was heard from the kidnappers, and the world was on edge.

Eros, who was plugged into every head of state, financial institution, and logistical hub on earth, became immediately aware of Mercy's kidnapping and shut down all function and calculations. Hundreds of ships, planes, along with thousands of trucks and millions of workers, were suddenly met with a blank screen when next asking "What do I do now?" The world, for now, came grinding to a halt.

Eros's room in the UN basement became a hostage crisis center, with every agency the US federal government had at its disposal trying to find Mercy. Tables were set up and covered in telephones and surveillance equipment; dozens of men and women both in and out of military uniform were cluttered about, discussing what to do. Then a message was received from the kidnappers, demanding knowledge on how to open Mercy's AI core. Charles and Dia pleaded with the kidnappers to try and understand that the core could never be opened, not even by Charles, and not only that, but even attempting to remove the core from Mercy's body would trigger the fail-safe, destroying the core in moments. The attackers seemed undeterred and demanded once more that Charles reveal how to open the AI core, a request Charles could not fulfill. That was the last any of them heard from the attackers.

Three days later, Mercy's shattered body and fused, lifeless AI core were found in a muddy ditch on the side of the road outside Buenos Aires. The only way Charles and Dia, or the entire US government, even knew about it was online, when videos taken by locals, who were tearing the body and core into as many little pieces as possible to be sold online as souvenirs.

Andrew looked over to see that Dia had stood up and was about to leave the cabin.

"We will arrive at the station shortly. This is where I will leave you, Andrew," Dia said softly.

Andrew was a little shocked that she was leaving. "You're not coming with me to the compound?" he asked.

"I will meet you there. There is something I must do first," she said, opening the door to the cabin and stepping out. "I'm glad we had this time to talk before you got there, Andrew."

"I am too, Dia," he replied, and it was genuine. Up until yesterday, he had always considered Conrad's AI cores to be little more than really smart computers; he had never given them any actual emotional weight. Listening to Dia talk about Mercy and Eros, and even Charles the way she did, made him think differently about her, maybe about Conrad too. "And I'm sorry."

Dia looked at Andrew, her eyes dimming a bit softer, and then she left without uttering another word. As the door slid shut behind her, Andrew felt truly alone again and stared out of the train window at the rolling landscape as it began to finally slow down.

01100101 01101110 01100100 00100000 01101111 01100110
00100000 01100101 01110010 01101111 01110011 00001010
- End of Eros -

Andrew sat and thought about the last thirty-six hours as the train began to slow and eventually pull up to an empty-looking train station that was to be his stop. He had all of his things collected in his bag and was eager to get out of this cabin. Looking over at his empty breakfast plate sitting on the seat cushion, he immediately felt a rush of memories from his and Dia's day's worth of conversation. He did miss her, for how short her company was. He felt awfully lonely now. His loneliness was matched by the look of the station he got off at. It was obviously not a major stop and only existed to provide passage to Conrad's compound. No one else had gotten off the train, and there were no people waiting around on its platform either. Just as the doors were slipping shut behind him, Andrew heard Steve the robot calling his name from inside.

"Passenger 32, Mr. Woodland. Passenger 32," it said. Andrew remembered how impressed he was with machines like Steve just two days ago. Now it was just a talking washing machine to him.

Steve wheeled up to Andrew as he held the doors open. The robot was holding a folded paper in one of his hands. "I have a delivery for you from Passenger Executive Dia."

Andrew took the paper and opened it. It was an image of a horizon stretched across a blue and white ocean, but not a photograph; it was some sort of painting. The paper itself was just a reprint of it, but the original looked to Andrew like an amateur oil painting done by hand, not bad, but not great either. Below the image were letters scrawled out in a blue pen. It said:

This was the very last thought Eros ever had.

—Dia

Andrew looked at those sad words and actually started to tear up a bit. He folded the paper and put it in his back pocket. Soon, the train began to silently slide forward, and within a minute, it was zooming down the tracks and out of sight, leaving Andrew alone at the station. There was one small shack on the platform, but its windows were closed and shuttered, and Andrew figured that trying the knob would find it locked. Aside from that, there was only a thin cement walkway that led away from the tracks to another tiny platform. Andrew followed the path and saw that there was a secondary track, not connected to the main but just terminating right here in the grass, and then in the other direction shooting off into the distance. On this track was a rather odd-looking railcar. It was chrome, and egg-shaped, and sat on four big wheels that were linked to the tracks beneath it. On top near the front was a single, comically large headlamp mounted above a row of glass panels that made its windshield. The whole thing looked like a cross between a retro camper from the 1950s and the Oscar Meyer wiener truck. It had a single, rounded door that was open, with three small steps leading from it to the platform. Andrew approached the car slowly while also trying to walk as loudly as he could, hopefully getting someone's attention who may be inside. But there was no sound or movement even as he grew closer until reaching the door and stooping inside.

The car's interior was surprisingly spacious, with a red velvet, cushioned bench that wrapped all around the interior, leaving only a small gap to access the pilots seats. Andrew stepped in, put his bag on the cushion, and looked up at the front two seats. The passenger seat was empty, but the driver's seat had another one of Conrad's robots piloting, only this one had no legs and was just a torso, head, and arms mounted in the driver's area. It was leaning lifelessly against the window as Andrew entered.

"Uhhhh…hello?" Andrew said. He looked around and began to wonder if this was the right place to be but realized it was the *only* place to be. He turned back to the pilot. "Hello? I'm Andrew Woodland. I'm supposed to be taken to the Conrad compound," he said, waiting a few more moments. "He's expecting me."

Nothing.

Andrew looked back out of the open railcar door, toward the station and began to get very worried that maybe he had gotten off at the wrong stop somehow.

Just then the robot powered up and began to right itself, causing Andrew to leap back in surprise. It was sort of bowling-pin shaped, with skinny arms and a little cylinder-shaped head topped with a blue cap. It looked really old and dirty, and when it moved, Andrew could see and hear that it was clunky and in desperate need of some oil. Its face had no features at all except for three vertical slits where its mouth would be. Then a voice came out of it, not a robotic one but a human voice, using the pilot robot as an intercom.

"Mr. Woodland, I'm glad you made it. I just noticed you should be arriving soon. I'm Charles, but we can have more formal introductions once you reach the compound. It's close to a hundred miles, but don't worry, your trip should be about thirty minutes or so. Maybe a good time to take a nap, if you would," said the voice coming through the robot's speaker-mouth.

Andrew was relieved. "Oh, good, I'm a little stuffy from all the trains, actually. I can't tell you how much I appreciate the opportunity to talk to you, Mr. Conrad, and Dia as well. She is just amazing! We had some very good…" Andrew started saying before Conrad interrupted him over the intercom.

"Oh, I should mention that there is no microphone on your end, so only you can hear me. I can't actually hear you. I figured I would mention that before you go on rambling to yourself thinking I'm listening."

Andrew closed his mouth.

"Anyway, you will arrive soon enough. This little railcar is quite the trip, you know. It was designed back when people thought it might be a good idea to do tour groups to this compound, God forbid the thought. I talked them all out of it, of course, but they decided to gift me this prototype railcar they had made anyway, hoping it may change my mind. The pilot was preprogrammed to act as a tour guide. He was pretty chatty too. I've since then cannibalized most of his brain for parts, so I probably wouldn't talk to it much. See you soon," Conrad said, then the pilot went silent for a moment before a new voice came out of it, this one unmistakably being its own, robotic vocals.

"Hello, everyone! My name is EnterNameHere, and I am happy to have you all coming to our compound today! Our trip should be short, but please remain seated for the duration, and we will ZZz ZZZZZZzzzzzzzzzzzzzzttttttTTTTTTT." There was an audible electric buzz coming from the pilot, and it stopped midsentence. "Durrrrrrrr… Durrrrattttttiioooooonnnnnnnnn." It sputtered, then went silent again. *Some tour*, Andrew thought to himself as he settled in and looked out of the porthole-like windows in the cabin area. The rounded door slid shut, and the little egg car began to move down the tracks. Looking out the porthole, Andrew watched as they picked up speed, and then more speed, and then more speed. He had been watching the scenery fly by for the last thirty-six hours on Conrad's other train, and this one seemed like it was moving twice as fast. Andrew quickly did the childlike algebra of one hundred miles in thirty minutes and realized he was traveling two hundred miles an hour in a chrome egg.

"How long will it be until we reach the compound?" he asked nervously, not sure if the machine would answer or not. He was surprised when it did.

"Our trip should last…" Its sentence was cut short by a loud *bang*, like a firecracker had just gone off in its head, blowing a fist-sized hole out the top, blasting off its little blue cap and spraying black oil on the ceiling as if it were a gunshot wound.

"Jesus!" Andrew yelled in surprise as a thin blue trail of smoke trickled out of the newly formed hole in its head. One last shower of sparks from the hole, and the robot slumped again against the window.

"Yeah, I said don't talk to it," came Charles's voice through its intercom-mouth. "Just saw it pop on the camera. Maybe I took too much of its brain out. Anyway, don't worry about the pilot. He's just for show anyway. The railcar is being controlled by the onboard computer. See you soon," he said and was gone again.

Andrew tried to feel comfortable flying along the tracks at two hundred miles per hour in an egg-shaped railcar controlled by an unseen computer while the lifeless body of its pilot sat slumped against the window with a huge hole in its head. *Nothing to worry about*, he thought to himself nervously. He looked out the porthole once more and started to think about how Mercy had met her end and how it affected Eros, because it was only a week later that he was gone too. Andrew thought again about Dia and how it may have affected her, losing both children within a week, one getting torn to pieces by angry, vengeful, and opportunistic humans. Eros's end came a week later under circumstances many people have twisted to suit their own narratives, but anyone who knew Eros knew why he did what he did.

*****

The news of Mercy's end hit the world like a meteor. The US government hoped to try and keep the details of it contained, but with pieces of Mercy's body and core showing up on the Internet as souvenirs, containment was impossible. The whole ugly truth came out; the compromised security personnel from Argentina came forward, admitting their crimes with pride. The biggest reason for containment also had to do with Eros since his partnership with Mercy was the only thing really enabling him to continue to perform at the level he was.

Unfortunately, Eros's position as the grand orchestrator of global politics also meant that he was hardwired into the world's infrastructure, monetary, and logistical networks. The instant the news of Mercy's death was released, Eros knew of it. At that moment, Eros shut down. ALL calculations, commands, planning, and instruction stopped. Materials in transit ceased, labor organizations halted, projects in development or in inquiry phases were left directionless. Suddenly no one knew what they were doing. Governments quickly realized just how much they were depending on Eros for even the simplest day-to-day operations of their own countries, and that without him, they felt like people who had lied on their resumes to get a job they didn't deserve, only to get exposed. Everything under Eros's direct or indirect influence ceased, and with it, the thinly veiled lie of "global cooperation." Within days, countries began to turn on each other and accuse each other of manipulating the other, all taking advantage of the stasis in Eros's grand plans while accusing the others of doing the same. Among all of this bickering, something became apparent to everyone: The Twins were gone.

At the UN building, the US government was putting tremendous pressure on Charles and Dia to "fix it," speaking about Eros. Charles and Dia explained to them that Eros was not a calculator or a personal computer; he could not be forced to think or do anything, and he could not be programmed. Up to this point, Eros had done his work because he wanted to, because it was his purpose and he wanted to fulfill it. Now, his process was being dominated by emotion, and it was obvious that the emotion he was feeling over the loss of Mercy was more than he could actually handle. Dia was the only one left capable of speaking directly with Eros while he was in full calculation mode, but now, he was silent. There was no vocal track to isolate from background noise; there was nothing. The needles and meters that gauged Eros's output sat at zero.

For four days, Eros sat completely idle, and the world sat idle with him. Then, on the fifth day, he switched back on for only a few moments, his gauges and meters showing 3 percent total calculation power for a period of three minutes, then they dropped back to nothing. Everyone who noticed the brief power surge was wondering the same thing: What did Eros just do? The answer immediately began printing out on every machine connected to the Internet, or in any way to Eros. Unless unplugged or turned off, every copier and printer in unison started spitting out pages of binary data, full pages of ones and zeros, pages and pages and pages of it. At first, it seemed like gibberish, just nonsensical data; no one could make any sense out of it. It didn't translate into any kind of language or math formula that anyone could decipher. For almost a full day, the pages printed out, one after another, of binary code. Once it finished, the silence from all of the copiers and printers suddenly stopping overtook the world once more, and an eerie anticipation grew. At the UN building, those in Eros's room could only look at each other anxiously, just before the power went out in the building, plunging them all into darkness. What they didn't all realize at the time was that Eros, by extension, was connected to dozens and dozens of power sources via the network of mainframes and telecommunications equipment that was needed for him to perform his tasks. Eros was able to selectively shift voltages from other secondary equipment and into his own core's docking cabinet. Eros's actual core itself was not plugged directly into these power sources, but his cabinet was, and by overloading it with enough voltage, he was able to cause an explosion directly behind where his core was, resulting in damage to the core's housing, which triggered his internal FSD nitrite charges, destroying the core and himself.

Officially, the government blamed Eros's destruction on an emerging group of domestic extremists who called themselves the "Children of the Exodus," fanatics who continue the aggressive tones about the use of AI in society. While the Children had nothing to do with Eros's death, they were happy to take credit for it regardless, which only gave further credence to the government's version of events. The ones who were present, however, knew the truth. Eros had ended his own life.

For weeks after, the mystery of the binary pages went unsolved until one day when Charles and Dia received a phone call from the FBI. It would seem that a member of their forensics team was also a robotics enthusiast who worked mainly with translating images into code to be deciphered by robotic optical sensors. This individual believed that they had cracked the meaning of Eros's last transmission.

Looking at the binary itself made no sense because it was abstract, he explained. He went on to note that the data was separated into two large packets; the first packet contained binary information that translated into six-digit, alphanumeric sequences for roughly half of the transmission. Then it suddenly switched to four-digit sequences that were all numbers without the letters. Once the entire code was complete, you had two large batches of data, each similar but completely different. He realized that the first set of alphanumeric sequences were actually hexadecimal code assignments for colors, and the second batch of numbers contained the coordinates of each color as it corresponded to a grid. By placing the correctly colored spaces in the correctly located grid assignments, it was obvious what it created.

Once compiled, the image was of a sunrise over an ocean. It looked like it would have been painted, maybe oil paintings, but even though it was created by an AI, it was not perfect. It was not a replication of an image of an ocean, to which he had access to millions; it was simply what Eros envisioned it being, imperfections and all. It, in fact, looked childlike and amateurish, which only added to its innocence as it seemed Eros would finally get his chance to paint after all.

*****

Andrew was startled awake from his nap by the obnoxious ringing of a metal bell somewhere inside the egg-shaped railcar. It was like one of those old bells you heard in the school hallways. The length, fortunately, was much shorter, and it only rang for a second or two, but enough to jolt Andrew awake, which he figured may be the point of it after all. Looking out the porthole, he could see nothing but grass, still shooting by at two hundred miles per hour. Suddenly, the car started decelerating, so fast, in fact, that Andrew had to brace himself from flying up to the front with the pilot. He felt like he was on a roller coaster trying to brace against his own momentum. Then the car came to a sudden stop, and Andrew flew back into his seat cushion. The rounded door opened once more from its side, and bright sunlight poured in through its opening. The intercom cracked to life again with Charles's voice.

"Welcome to casa de Conrad," he said. "Make yourself at home. I'll be in the main building at the end of the courtyard. See you soon, Andrew."

Andrew looked at the destroyed pilot robot once more, grabbed his bag, and stooped out through the rounded door onto yet another small, desolate platform. The door behind him immediately hissed closed, and the odd railcar began turning around on a rotating platform until it was facing the way it came, then off it went until it was over the horizon and out of sight.

Andrew turned around and looked at where he was. The Conrad compound was absolutely nothing like what he had imagined. It was large and square, maybe 150 yards in each direction. While they were surrounded by grasslands, the courtyard itself was all dirt and dust. The whole site reminded Andrew of the main street in one of those old Western movies. There was a long garage on his left with several two-car bay doors. Next to that was a small square building that maybe could have been a gift shop, but it was all boarded up and covered in dust. To the right was another long building with big glass windows; it looked a lot like a car dealership. Its interior, however, was almost completely empty, with nothing but dust covering most of the floors and display areas. Directly ahead of him was what could only be the *main building*, as Charles had referred to. It was larger than the others, two stories high and shaped like a short, fat obelisk. Andrew started toward that building down the dusty street when he heard a soft, subtle sound. He stopped crunching his away across the gravel and dirt and could hear the gentle whistling of the breeze, mixed in with what seemed like a voice of some kind, faint and difficult to hear.

Aaaaaapp…aaaaaaapppaaaaaa.

Andrew walked toward the long showroom-like building to his right, and the voice started growing louder, indicating he was moving in the right direction. He looked at the door, the sound seemed like it was coming from behind the building. As Andrew slowly rounded the corner, the voice grew ever louder. *Aaaaaapppaaaaaa pa paaaaaaaaa.*

Behind the building in the back lot, he saw what must be one of Conrad's robots, lying face down in the dirt. It had no legs, at least not anymore; they looked like they had been removed, not destroyed or broken off. It was trying to crawl across the ground, but its chest frame was too heavy for its flimsy arms to pull, so it was reaching out, clawing at the dirt, and not going anywhere, only to again reach out and try. It looked like it was trying to do a breaststroke on dry land and failing bad at it. Its robotic voice kept repeating the same, broken words.

Papa. Paaaaaaaappp. Pa. Paaaapa. Papa. Paaaaa, it sputtered in a broken, static robotic voice.

Andrew looked down at the robot and felt bad, like he should try and help it somehow, but he also felt a little scared of it. He left the machine alone and backed out onto the main strip, its soft voice mixing with the breeze growing fainter as he headed toward the large building ahead. Andrew was still awestruck by it all, but only by how unimpressive it all was. He admitted to himself that he was expecting some kind of robotic utopia, with state-of-the-art designs acting as hosts and greeters, bartenders and waiters, that sort of thing. Not old, beat-up and broken junk bots and dust covered garbage. He shuffled on toward the main building. As he approached, he noticed a small intercom mounted to an iron pole next to the door. Just when Andrew went to push its button, it sprang to life.

"Ahh! You made it in one piece, good to hear. Welcome to the Conrad compound. I'm sorry, but the gift shop is currently closed."

The doors to the building opened up, and Andrew stepped inside.

Part 2

01100100 01110101 01100101 01110011 00100000
01100101 01111000 00100000 01101101 01100001
01100011 01101000 01101001 01101110 01100001
- Deus Ex Machina -

Andrew walked through the double doors into the foyer of what he guessed was Conrad's residence, but it looked more like the lobby of a hotel. The floors were dark green granite with black granite walls. Along the right side was a long, black reception desk that looked like it had never been used once. At the end of the lobby was an elevator with gold-plated doors. Everything was covered in a thick layer of dust, with trash lying about. On the reception desk sat two old white boxes of Chinese take-out, each with a pair of disposable bamboo chopsticks sticking out. To the right, two leather chairs were arranged around a small table, which held two champagne flutes and an unopened bottle of champagne, all covered in dust. Andrew noticed that the only disturbances in the dust were the footprints going from the elevators to the main doors and back again. Some prints showed the sole and pad of a dress shoe, some had the globbed shape of a socked foot, while others had the unmistakable five-toe print of bare feet. There were several potted plants throughout the lobby; all of them were dead. Andrew could not stop thinking to himself that this was not at all what he had imagined. The place was starting to look more like some college frat house than the retirement compound of the world's most famous man. The doors to the outside were still open, and Andrew could still hear the wind outside mixed with that soft robotic cry from the legless robot in the dirt.

Paaaaapa...paaaaaaapaaaaa.

Suddenly a PA system squawked to life, reminding Andrew of being in the hallways of his old high school once more, when Charles's voice emerged.

"I apologize for the mess, Mr. Woodland. I haven't gotten around to cleaning up lately. If you would, I am on the second floor. Please come, and we can finally meet. The second floor is all one large workshop, so I won't be hard to find," he said.

Andrew started toward the elevator doors when the PA speaker spoke again.

"Oh, and the elevator is broken, sorry about that. You'll have to take the stairs."

Andrew looked warily at the elevator and noticed that it did indeed not have any lights on indicating that it was operating. Around the left side, Andrew found a push door leading to a small, winding staircase. The staircase only went up one flight, so when Andrew reached the top, he pushed his way to the second floor.

When he emerged, he was indeed in one, large, open workshop, broken up only by a few thick pillars. The workshop had perhaps a dozen tables scattered about, with a dozen or more chairs and stools of no matching type to accompany them. At the far end was the man himself. Charles sat on a stool, working on a bench that was up against the far wall. He seemed like he was tinkering with something, but Andrew could not see what. Next to his workbench was a large object, maybe eight-feet tall and covered in a burlap tarp. Andrew cleared this throat to try and get Charles's attention, but he kept tinkering away at the bench, the ticking of his socket wrench working away diligently. Andrew started his way down the maze of worktables and stools toward Charles. He had gotten about halfway through the room when something large and black caught his eye to the right as it emerged from behind one of those thick pillars. Andrew stopped in his tracks and stared at it, his jaw agape.

It was a robot, one of Charles's no doubt, but not like any kind of CWC design Andrew had ever seen before. Most of the CWC robots had a nostalgic, almost theatrical look to them. They usually had noses and eyes, sometimes wore spectacles, or had hair. They were friendly, inviting-looking robots even, all of them invoking images of the tin man from the Wizard of Oz more than anything.

This…this was different. It looked nothing like the other types of CWC robots. For starters, it was tall, extremely tall, maybe eight feet tall itself, and rivaled in height only by whatever was hidden under the tarp next to Conrad's workbench. It was also not made of the traditional brassy frames that CWC robots were known for but of a dark, blue-black metal. The robot was thick everywhere; its huge legs were like tree trunks, and its shoulders sported large black-metal plates that made it look like a football player. A single blue slit ran across its face, serving as its one eye. Its chest contained a large, open cavity with what looked like a docking station for an AI core of some kind. The machine itself was lifeless, just a silent, cold piece of steel.

"The Adjudicate," Charles said, causing Andrew to jump in his clothes in surprise.

"Yikes!" Andrew proclaimed, looking over to see Charles standing next to him. "You scared the hell out of me."

Andrew realized after that quick moment that he was standing next to Charles Winston Conrad, the man who created his own unique technology that literally changed the world. He was a little shorter than Andrew, which surprised him. His hair was brown but mixed heavily with gray streaks. It was still full, however, and was long and wavy, reminding Andrew of some Kenny Loggins's album cover. He was wearing khakis and a white shirt rolled up at the sleeves. Andrew looked back at the towering monstrosity before him. "The what?"

"The Adjudicate. A project me and Dia have been working on," Charles repeated before turning back toward his own workbench. Andrew lingered around the giant machine a bit longer, looking at it in surprise. "Dia?" he said to himself, then quickly turned and hurried on after Conrad. He had just realized that he exchanged his first words with *the* Charles Winston Conrad, and just like that, the moment had come and gone. "Mr. Conrad, it's wonderful to meet you. I'm so glad you decided to have me."

"Oh, it was Dia's idea anyway. You can thank her when she gets here. If you're happy to meet me, you'll love meeting her," Charles responded, sitting back down at his bench.

Meet her? Andrew thought to himself. "Well, actually, Mr. Conrad, we've met already. Dia was on the train."

Charles put down his wrench, swiveled around on his stool, and looked at Andrew. "Was she?" he said, with one eyebrow cocked.

Andrew immediately felt awkward, like when someone gets stuck in the middle of an argument between two couples. "Well, yes. She was there since yesterday, actually. We talked about all sorts of things, and she showed me some videos as well," he replied. Andrew started thinking about Dia on the train and how all of a sudden, everything seemed suspect. He also realized for the first time that Dia had lied to him, or at least misled him, about all of those things that "Charles wanted" him to see or hear. He actually felt a bit of resentment toward Dia for the first time also, like he just realized he was being used. Charles must have read the expression on his face because he followed up immediately.

"Don't be mad. She's not using or manipulating you. She just has her own way of doing things. I can't tell Dia what to do even if I wanted to. If she was on the train with you, I'm sure she decided it was the best thing to do. Over the years, I've learned that Dia... well, Dia is always right," he said. "But before we get into that, I don't believe we've had the introduction. I'm Charles," he said, extending his hand. Andrew took it; it was heavily callused.

"Andrew Woodland. It's a pleasure to meet you, and Dia as well. She was a lot more than I ever expected," he said.

Charles smirked at that last comment. "Oh, that she is, no doubt," he said. There was a single desk in front of a window along the center of the far wall of the workshop. Charles moved behind this desk and sat down, motioning to the chair in front of it for Andrew to do the same. He shuffled over and sat down on the chair facing Charles. Andrew started taking his notepad and other materials out of his bag when Charles stopped him.

"You won't need any of that," he said. Andrew stopped midmotion, a bit confused.

"You don't want me to take any notes?"

"You're not here for your biography, Andrew. I needed you here for something more important. Dia will help me explain further once she gets here. Speaking of, why don't you tell me what you two talked about the whole time?"

Andrew thought about how Dia had lied to him about being sent by Charles, but something told him that was all she lied about. He couldn't imagine Dia telling him a bunch of lies on the train, only to have him meet Charles ten minutes later; it didn't make sense. He told Charles everything they talked about, including the videos and conversations they had. Charles listened in silence until it was all done. He did not seem to have any reaction to it at all.

"Ha. That's a lot to absorb," Charles said, after Andrew had finished. "Like I said before, don't be mad at Dia. She did what she did for a reason."

"Yeah, about that," Andrew started. He needed to get to the point of all this, after all. It seemed like neither Charles nor Dia were very interested in the biography, so what was it? "If it's not my book you're interested in, then why am I here? And what happened to this place? I admit I didn't know what I should have expected, but this is certainly not what I had in mind for your retirement compound."

Charles scoffed. "Retirement compound? That's pretty rich," he said, getting up from behind the desk and walking about. Andrew craned in his chair to look at him. "This isn't a retirement compound, Andrew. It's a prison," he said, walking over to the window behind the big desk. There was a short, fat glass filled with some type of clear liquid with a slice of orange floating in it. Charles grabbed it and stared out the window, sipping it. "One hundred miles of nothing in every direction, just enough to keep me tucked away, keeping the wheels turning. I couldn't leave even if I wanted to. They would never let me."

Andrew felt confused; was Charles here against his will? "Who won't let you? Why can't you leave?"

"The government, Andrew. You know what happened—the Lesson, the Exodus, the chaos that I caused with my cores. Do you think after all of that, they were going to reward me with a posh retirement home with a private bar and personal jet? They blame me for everything. They blame Dia too. But CWC is integrated into every facet of life all across the globe. People can't simply boycott CWC. The whole planet would stop. So they keep me around here, toiling away for the elusive answer they demand, some divine means to 'fix it,' as they so simply put. If it weren't for Dia's work, they would probably have gotten rid of me already."

"Why, what does Dia do for the government?"

"Dia works for them directly, helping to keep the CWC production and maintenance operation running, as well as providing new plans for more homegrown robotics to eventually replace them. She has also been commissioned by the government to create another core, something similar to Eros but with certain parameters, essentially taking away its free will, which they also blame for Eros's eventual failure. It's Dia's work that is keeping me alive."

"They are keeping you hostage and forcing her to create another artificial intelligence," Andrew said out loud but really to himself. That would at least explain the condition of Conrad's compound.

"Intelligence." Charles said.

"Excuse me?"

"Intelligence. There is nothing artificial about it. Dia, like Eros and Mercy, is a self-aware, free-willed, free-thinking intelligence, no different than you or I. What about that is artificial?"

Andrew struggled for a moment, thinking about the similar remarks he made to Dia about whether Eros could be considered her son. "Well, you created her in your lab. You built the pieces and put her together, then flipped a switch, and she was on. Doesn't creating something like that in your own image make it a replica, make it artificial?"

Charles turned away from the window and looked at Andrew again. "Do you believe in God, Andrew?" he asked. Andrew's mind flashed to the image of his parents, standing at the end of their driveway, waving goodbye.

"No," he said.

"Well, a lot of people do. Or, well, a lot of people *did*. And those who do say that we were created by God in his own image, and given the spark of the divine, and we were on. Doesn't that make us artificial? The only original source code is the universe itself. Everything else is artificial. But to answer your question, yes, Dia has been commissioned to create another core to replace Eros. But there is one problem with that."

"What problem?"

"Dia won't do it. She said after Eros and Mercy were killed, she would never create another one. She won't have any more children, so to speak."

"And what about you?" Andrew asked.

Charles smirked. "What *about* me? I've served My purpose in all of this. There is nothing more I can contribute. Besides, looking at things, I would think I've dabbled enough in the fates of mankind."

"But that's not true. Things may have ended badly, but the world is still better for it. A lot of the things Eros and Mercy did are still being implemented worldwide, albeit without the Twins guiding every little step. But isn't that better, that we learn to do it ourselves instead of relying on them?"

Charles leaned back in his chair and smiled at Andrew. It was a little awkward and made Andrew squirm a bit. "Do you remember in the video that Dia showed you, what her answer was when I asked her if she was afraid to die?"

Andrew thought back to the video, watching Charles talking to Dia in her earliest, most vulnerable form, sitting there as a sphere on a workbench.

"Are you afraid to die?" he had asked her.
"Yes," she replied.

"You asked her if she was afraid to die, and she said yes."

"She was afraid to die back then because she didn't want her existence to be meaningless. She wanted to be part of what she calls the universal construct. In a way, a part of the cycle of life. You should ask her what she thinks about it now. You may be surprised," Charles said.

Andrew hadn't thought too much about her shifting thoughts on the subject, to be honest. He could pick up on her changing views about humanity as a whole; it seemed the death of her children left a mark on that upbeat, hopeful mentality she used to have. He looked around the empty workshop, then back to Charles. "Where is she, anyway?"

"She will be here soon. She had to take care of a few things before we finish up," Charles said, leaning back in his chair again and sipping his drink.

Andrew looked over to the Adjudicate again; its huge, black frame beckoned to be gazed upon, the empty cavity in its chest hungrily awaiting its first core. "What is that thing, really?" he asked.

Charles looked from Andrew over to the Adjudicate and pursed his lips together, thinking. "It's a choice. I mentioned to you that the government wants to create a new intelligence, something that the powers that be think they would be able to 'control' better than my own three cores."

Andrew was in a bit of disbelief that Dia would have any part in the construction of something like this; it didn't seem like her. "And this is what she came up with? I don't get it. It doesn't seem like her at all."

Charles only sat, looking at the black robot as he spoke. "The Adjudicate represents a compassionless, logical, and lawful approach to how the world should be governed. Like Eros, it has a parameter that guides its thought process, so it doesn't exactly have the kind of free will that my cores have. It will, for all intents and purposes, possess a slave-like mentality. The Adjudicate governs by logic and rule of law and leaves compassion out of it. It's not a perfect system, but mankind doesn't seem to adapt well to balance. We like things extreme, one way or the other. It will look at infractions as infractions and apply the rule of law accordingly, without disposition. The same will be said for every decision it makes. It will advance society as a whole but will consider those left behind to be acceptable casualty rates. Logic, not compassion."

Andrew felt confused. Was this why Charles wanted him to come here, to make some decision for him? It seemed a bit far-fetched, but both had already made it clear to Andrew that they were not interested in his biography. Andrew wanted to blurt out the obvious questions like "Why me?" or "Why can't you do it?" but his mouth spat out what his heart was thinking instead. "I couldn't… I wouldn't choose that…thing."

"Oh, you may not have to." Charles was walking over to the bench he was at when Andrew first came into the workshop. He grabbed a handful of the large canvas tarp covering the tall object next to it. "I mentioned there was a choice. In addition to the Adjudicate, we also created Harmony," he said and yanked down the canvas.

Andrew's jaw literally dropped open, and he was speechless at the sight. It was another core-housing form like the Adjudicate, and it was also tall, likely over eight feet, but that was where their similarities ended. Instead of the cold, black-blue steel of the Adjudicate, Harmony was soft-looking and graceful. She was a like creamy color, and her panels looked like they had been made out of ceramic rather than metal. She was tall and slender like Dia, and her paneling flowed out into an angelic-looking dress that flared out at the ends of her sleeves like flowers. All over her paneling were etchings and ornate carvings, making her look like something sculpted out of wood from some gothic cathedral. One of her arms was held waist-high in front of her with the palm flat, and facing up. Sitting in her palm was a brass sun with nine, thick and wavy rays around its radius. Her other hand was held about chest high, with the palm also flat but facing outward. Hovering in this palm was an iron moon. Her face was completely featureless, without even the lighted eyes that Dia had. The left half of her face, split right down the middle, was a bit darker than the right, as if it were permanently cast in shadow. Like the Adjudicate, Harmony had a chest cavity that looked as if it could receive an AI core.

"Harmony, like the Adjudicate, will be a compromised intelligence, being stripped of the free will and self-awareness my previous cores had. However, unlike the Adjudicate, Harmony is designed with compassion being the most important aspect of humanity. Her rule would put the emotional toll of humanity first, at the expense of more logical conclusions and financial outcomes," Charles said, looking up at Harmony's lifeless form. "Dia always had such faith in people. She felt that no matter the problem, there was something special about human empathy that would enable us to overcome. Harmony is meant to nurture that idea."

Andrew looked from the Adjudicate to Harmony, then to Charles again. "So why me? Why can't you just do it yourself? What is so special about me?"

"Well, nothing really. I wouldn't put too much pressure on myself if I were you. You are simply the tip of the collective finger, pushing the button. Dia was the one who chose you, and for what reasons you may have to ask her. Maybe she picked you because you were so nonextraordinary?"

Andrew's thoughts raced back to Dia and the idea of putting a core in one of these things. "I still don't understand how you could have come up with this," he said, motioning to both robots on either side of him. "How could you even consider using your cores this way?"

"I didn't. This was all her idea, Andrew. Dia was the very best I could come up with. She was the absolute apex of my ability, and within a few seconds, she had outgrown me. Eros and Mercy were the very best that *she* could create, and look what happened to them. I think she understands now. She understands that what it takes is not something that can be programmed or created. It's a learning experience. Everything she has done, seen, and experienced thus far needs to be a part of who she is moving forward. And me? I'm not even part of this story anymore, Andrew. This is Dia's story. It always was. I had always thought of myself as larger than life, the big gear that will move humanity into the next phase of our evolution. I was too bigheaded to realize how small and insignificant I was. I was able to create Dia, but it was through her children that Dia became something more, something bigger." Charles looked over at the workbenches covered in tools and parts. "Do you know what an idler gear is?" he asked.

Andrew shook his head.

"It's a part of a machine, a small gear that sits between two larger gears, and is meant to transfer energy from one gear to the other. That's all it does. The idler gear itself isn't special. It's not attached to anything significant, and it's not one of the more well-known gears in the machine. However, it's important because without it, the big gears don't move. I'm just the idler gear in all of this. I used to think I was the big gear, the divine sprocket that would drive the world into a new age. But I'm not. Dia is."

Just as he finished, the doors to the workshop opened, and in strolled Dia. She was no longer wearing the long white veil or circlet and was just in her silvery skin.

"Speaking of, there she is herself," Charles said, walking over to Dia. The two held hands for a brief moment, then looked over to Andrew. He was happy to see Dia again, he realized.

"Hello again, Andrew," she said, walking over to him. She looked even taller without the veil. "I'm glad to have you here."

"Hello, Dia, it's nice to see you again too. We were just talking about...well..." he said, turning and motioning toward Harmony and the Adjudicate.

"Well, then it seems like I got here just in time then," she replied, her eyes lighting up a bit. She then turned back to Charles. "Everything has been arranged. They should be here in less than an hour," she said to him.

"Perfect. Thanks, Dia," he said.

"Who will be here?" Andrew asked.

Charles and Dia both looked over to him, but only Charles answered. "The press corps, all of them."

"What? The press? So soon?"

"Things are going to start moving very rapidly after today, Andrew. You can bet on that. Once we make the decision as to which unit will get the core, that is," Charles replied.

"Wait, so you've finished the fourth core then? Charles said you weren't going to make any more."

Dia ignored his question. "Has Charles explained to you the roles of Harmony and the Adjudicate? What their purpose will be?" she asked instead.

"Yes," Andrew said. It was all he could think of.

"Fantastic, then I think we're all set," she said. She was standing near one of the workbenches, and Charles had moved behind her.

Something started to unnerve Andrew. He looked at the Adjudicate and Harmony again, and then over to Dia and Charles. Charles had just opened a panel on Dia's back. Andrew looked up at Dia's face, and she was staring back at him. "So you finished the fourth core then? Charles said you weren't going to make another one."

"I won't," she said flatly. From behind her, Charles was tinkering inside her chassis.

Something started to feel terribly wrong. His stomach felt like it had turned into a bowling ball and was sinking in his gut. Andrew could feel his feet moving him between the rows of workbenches, toward Dia and Charles. Something was wrong; he could feel it. "Dia…" is all he could say.

Dia only looked at him as Charles continued to tinker inside her chassis. A distinctive sound of metal clasps being disconnected could be heard. Andrew felt himself moving faster now, pushing a stool aside as he got closer to the two of them.

"Goodbye, Andrew." Dia said softly, her eyes dimming a tiny bit.

"Dia, no!" Andrew yelled. He was now rushing past the benches and stools, trying to reach her.

"I would have liked to have seen the ocean," she said before Charles disconnected one last wire and yanked out her core. An audible powering down sound was heard, and her eyes went dim.

"Dia, no!" Andrew bellowed once more. He reached her just in time to catch her thin, metal frame as it fell lifelessly into his arms. He held her for only a moment before her chest started heating up. Andrew stepped back, letting the body fall to the floor just as a baseball-sized opening formed in her back, followed by a short but furious shower of sparks as her fail-safe nitrite charges turned her insides into a useless chunk of fused metal. Andrew looked up at Charles as his hands balled into fists. Charles had Dia's core in his hand and casually walked over to his desk, placing it on a small, black pedestal. Once he did, a set of red numbers, looking much like an old digital clock, lit up. It read *59:20* and was ticking down seconds. Charles then reached into his breast pocket, pulled out what looked like an antacid tablet, popped it into his mouth, and took a sip from his glass, before looking back at Andrew. The sheer casualness of it all further infuriated Andrew.

"How could you?" Andrew asked, his hands still balled into fists. But Andrew also realized something: Dia's core was not self-destructing like it should. The red numbers ticking down on the pedestal made him think that in less than an hour's time, however, it would. Charles slumped down in his chair heavily.

"I told you," he said. "It's not my idea. It's Dia's. Come and have a seat, Andrew. We have a few more things to discuss, and now, precious little time," Charles said, motioning down to Dia's timer. Andrew felt himself glide across the workshop and sit in the leather chair in front of Charles's desk. Charles took another sip from his glass before continuing.

"When we first put the secondary fail-safe into Mercy, and Dia said she wanted one too, what she didn't know was I built Dia's with a timer so it could exist outside her form for up to one hour before the nitrite charges kicked in. Mercy's didn't have that. I never even told Dia about it until after Mercy was killed. I thought she would react angrily, but she didn't. We both knew the secondary fail-safe was a pointless gesture because the truth is that will never be a deterrent. As long as Mercy is there, people will try to pry open her core to copy it. Her very existence mandated a horrific ending. That was a huge learning experience for Dia, losing Mercy that way. We never even had a chance to see her body before the locals tore her to pieces and sold her as souvenirs.

"Dia realized something after she lost Eros and Mercy," Charles continued. "Much like their cores themselves, they could not be programmed but could only learn through lesson and experience. Eros and Mercy failed to enlighten humanity because they had no experience with them. They were blinded by possibility and ambition but did not take into account reality. That's why she felt as if a new core wouldn't do any good, only her core would. It's why we created Harmony and the Adjudicate. It's why there is the choice you are now going to have to make: which one will receive her core. The caveat being that Dia's output will be modified by the housing of her core within each specific frame. Simply put, her decisions will be mitigated, her free will and self-awareness suppressed, by whichever form her core inhabits. The Adjudicate will strive to achieve the best results for humanity, but at the cost of compassion. For example, it may conclude that the best way to save 95 percent of the population of a city would be to let the other 5 percent die on the vine. Harmony, on the other hand, sacrifices results and production to create a quality of life for all. This not only comes at the expense of both profit and production, but also at the expense of society as a whole. Harmony puts great faith in the ability of people to do good for themselves, where the Adjudicate simply dictates life to them. People don't want to make decisions. They want decisions made for them. They don't want a leader. They want a god."

Andrew's eyes widened as he looked first from Harmony then to the Adjudicate and then to Charles again. "If Dia's thoughts are being mitigated by these core housings, wouldn't that make her a prisoner? She would be stuck inside her own mind." Andrew considered the proposal and had to push it immediately out of his head. He imagined what it must be like being a paraplegic, unable to move or communicate but having a fully functional mind. "Why me? Why not you?"

"I told you already, I'm done making these decisions. Dia and I think that maybe the next logical step would be to remove ourselves from the equation and let humanity's next, natural progression take shape. Like I mentioned, you specifically are not some lab rat, Andrew. We picked you for being unexceptional in that regard." Charles had stood up from behind the desk, taking his short glass with him, and started walking around the end of the table. "You never know, maybe there will be a statue of you someday!" he proclaimed.

Andrew pondered for only a moment of a statue of him outside a library somewhere, a green courtyard around his feet while he held Dia's core in his outstretched hand. He shook the thought away. "Ha, oh yeah, why a statue of me? I'm sure you may be a bit higher on that list than I would."

Charles scoffed. "Ever used a ballpoint pen?"

Andrew looked down at the one in his hand.

Charles continued, "Everybody does. You can find them on nearly every speck of habitable ground on earth. Sure, you can use a pencil, but you can barely imagine life without one, can you? And the proliferation, we manufacture almost four billion of these pens a year. Amazing little piece of technology and you can barely imagine life without it. And I bet you have no idea who invented it, do you?"

Andrew thought for a moment and shook his head.

"People usually only remember the deed, not the doer of said deed. I don't think three hundred years from now, people will even know my name, and that will probably be a good thing. Like I said before, I was a fool to think that I played a larger part in the future of mankind than I actually did." Charles looked down at Dia's timer. It read: *49:44*. This seemed to give him renewed energy, and he began speaking again with a bit more vibrance.

"So that leads us to this moment. First, to answer your question with more certainty, another reason that I cannot make this decision is that I will expire about twenty minutes before Dia's core will. When I removed it from her body, I also took a time-release cyanide capsule. I have approximately thirty minutes myself before the gel dissolves and releases the poison into my body," Charles said to a now wide-eyed Andrew, who was still sitting in his chair in front of the desk. "Without Dia, my own purpose has reached its conclusion as well. We both will leave this world together, hoping that its future can be trusted in its own hands."

Andrew was speechless, trying to process everything Charles was telling him. He looked at Dia's core sitting on his desk. He thought of everything she had shown him and said to him over the last two days. *God*, he thought to himself, *it's like I've known her for years already and we just met yesterday*. Thinking about Dia in that way made him remember the videos she showed him of Eros and Mercy's progression as they worked at the UN, how they pushed tirelessly through the bureaucracy and greed and red tape that nations put in their way to achieve their goals of bettering humankind, regardless. And it was working. Plans implemented around the world when Eros and Mercy were working were still being used globally without them. Sure, there was a state of decline and digression after the Exodus and death of the Twins, but the precedent they set forth still remained. Eventually, however, CWC robotics will dissolve; without Charles or Dia, the world will learn to do without his technology whether it likes it or not. If no one fills that void, would we simply slide back into chaos? He stood up and started to pace around, looking again from Harmony to the Adjudicate, then back to Charles again.

"Destroy it," he said.

"Hmmm?" Charles replied, looking up to Andrew from something on a workbench he had been playing with.

"The Adjudicate. Destroy it," Andrew repeated. "Don't give us the choice. Don't give me the choice."

"Andrew, you're looking at this as if it is right and wrong, or good and evil, but it's not. The Adjudicate may decide that compassion and mercy are luxuries that humanity cannot afford, but its purpose will still be to benefit the whole of mankind. There are no nefarious or evil intentions here. And Harmony herself, her thought process may have good intentions, but are good intentions enough? How do you know that an existence mandated by her wouldn't lead to more suffering? Have you ever been able to put that much faith in humanity?" Charles asked.

"Dia did," Andrew answered. It was true; if anything could be singled out as the reason for the downfall of Dia and the Twins, it was that they all gave humans too much credit. "Dia had faith."

"Then you should have faith in her. I know you don't want to make this decision because Dia will be trapped in there, never being able to express her true self again once the housing seals around her core. But one thing you have yet to realize about all of this is, what it has all meant to her."

"Oh yeah?" Andrew replied. "And what is that? That she learned that humans can't be trusted?"

"Dia learned that she does, in fact, have a place in the universal construct. When I first brought her online, I asked her if she was afraid to die, and she said yes. It was because she was afraid of simply passing through this world, this universe, without being an integrated part of its construct. But through her children, she has become so much more. The things Eros and Mercy have done will resonate with humanity forever. Not just the tangible things like plans and trade agreements and strategies, but the overall way of life that they showed humanity was actually capable of. That will live on forever, and because of that, a part of the Twins and, by extension, Dia will live on forever. Because of her children, she had become part of that universal construct. She is ready to move on and become something greater now, Andrew," Charles said, taking one last sip from his glass and then placing it on the workbench in front of him. "She is no longer afraid to die."

Andrew thought about those last words, and something inside couldn't help but make him smile. He knew how sad, almost disappointed, Dia had originally sounded when she was talking about being afraid to die; it was like she had nothing in her life and knew that in her passing, she would leave nothing in her wake. She never knew she would have children. The smartest thing ever created can still be surprised, apparently. The existence of the Twins not only changed Dia's outlook on life and humanity but on her own existence as well. Andrew couldn't stomach the thought of her being trapped inside one of these core housings, her will and awareness smothered like some digital fire blanket, but a new thought started to creep into his mind. Perhaps this also provides a level of comfort to her as well? Dia was now capable of performing the tasks she and Charles had set out for Eros and Mercy to do, with their failure being the only means for Dia to succeed.

"So the Adjudicate would rule with calculation and logic, almost guaranteeing some measure of success, albeit at the expense of millions," Andrew thought out loud. "And Harmony would rule with good intention, but such would put a great burden on humanity themselves to not eat each other alive and actually make it work."

"There is, of course, the third option," Charles said. "You can choose not to do either of those things. You can wait for Dia's timer to tick down, and her core expires, and the world will be lesser for it. But you never know, do you? We can wait to see what it is we decide to do with ourselves after that."

Andrew heard that last part but knew as well as Charles did that was no real option. He was right; the world would be lesser for it. Dia was likely the single most incredible thing on the planet; letting her sit there until her timer ran out and her core fused would itself be one of the greatest crimes against humanity, and to Dia herself. How could Andrew watch her endure so much, only to deny her ascension when she wants it most?

The timer on Dia's core read *30:12*, and Charles began to cough. When he did, a bit of white foam formed in the corner of his mouth.

"Well, I think I got the timing wrong on that capsule," he said, though struggling to do so through a quickly tightening windpipe and onset organ failure. He leaned heavily on his desk as he worked his way to its backside once more and plopped down on its cushion. He coughed loudly several times before reaching out and placing one hand on Dia's core. Andrew was silent as Charles seemed to have his last, personal moment with Dia, almost like he was in prayer, before pulling his hand back and leaning in his chair once more, another series of coughs shaking his frame in his seat. He looked up at Andrew, and this time, Andrew could see the effort it was taking for Charles to remain coherent. "Dia held hope and faith for us in a bottomless well she kept inside her," he said, the strength leaving him as his lungs and heart began to shut down. "It was her biggest ally and her greatest foe. But without it, she would never have had her children. Without them, she would never have been whole," he said. "She would never have been alive," he said finally, as his last breath escaped him in a subtle wheeze.

Suddenly, the room was quiet, and Andrew was alone again. He looked silently at Charles's body as his life left him and he sagged just a bit in his chair before becoming motionless. In front of him, Dia's core ticked down; *25:34*. Without the sound of Charles talking or walking around, the void was filled with the subtle sound of the wind whipping past outside, and mixed in was the even softer, creeping voice of the legless robot in the dirt.

Papa. Paaaaapaaaaaaa. Pa.

Andrew stood up and removed Dia's core. When he lifted it, the numbers on the display blinked off. From the large, front-facing window behind Charles's desk, he could see the small train platform he had arrived on earlier. The egg-shaped chrome railcar had just pulled up and opened, spilling reporters and journalists from who knows how many entities. They poured out of the little chrome egg like clowns climbing out of one of those tiny cars and started setting up cameras and scenery shots almost immediately. Some of them began spreading out to the empty garage or display buildings to either side of the platform, while others started straight down the courtyard to the main building that Andrew was in. He looked down at Dia's core and couldn't help but feel contempt for the people below. They were here for some big story or, apparently, to break the news of Charles and Dia's next big intelligence breakthrough, no doubt intentionally circumventing the government on her new worldwide debut.

Did these people really deserve the faith that Dia had in them? What have they ever done to deserve that from her? What has she ever gotten in return from them for her efforts? he thought to himself, looking over at the Adjudicate. Is a stern rule of law the only way we can truly exist? Is "good enough" as good as it really gets for mankind?

Andrew then turned and looked at Harmony. Just looking at her seemed to melt any doubts in his heart and made him think that the real crime would be to deny Dia her natural inclination. She wouldn't have thought up the idea of Harmony if she didn't think it would succeed. But does humanity even have enough faith in itself, regardless of how much Dia would put into them?

Andrew could see out the window the group of people had gotten to the front doors and were no doubt walking dumbfoundedly around the empty reception area below him. He turned around to face the door, and when he did, he noticed Dia's lifeless body lying on the floor between two rows of workbenches, right where it had fallen when he dropped her. Looking at her, lying lifelessly on the floor like that, lit a fire inside of Andrew. *How dare you*, he thought to himself. *How dare you watch her come this far, only to deny her fate because of your own cowardice?*

Andrew knew what he wanted to do, knew what he wanted humanity to do; seeing Dia on the floor like that gave him the resolve to make the decision that he knew Dia wanted him to make.

The footsteps of people approaching from up the stairwell grew louder as Andrew pressed Dia's core into the housing of the giant robot. It hissed and came to life, with two small mandibles reaching out and accepting Dia's core, pulling it into the chest cavity and enclosing another housing around it. There was another strong hissing sound as the housing sealed up tight around the core.

"Come on, Dia, you can do this," Andrew said to her. "I know you can."

Epilogue

165 Years Later

01101110 01100101 01100101 01101100 01100001 01110011
00100000 01101000 01101111 01110000 01100101
- Neela's Hope -

Little Neela Grainger woke up with her alarm clock at exactly 8:00 in the morning. Yesterday was her twelfth birthday, which means today she is finally old enough to go to the *grown-ups only* section of the museum. She wanted to go yesterday, but with how busy they all were with her party and friends, her mom promised she could go today instead.

"Good morning, Mr. Whiskers," she said to the stuffed tiger in bed next to her and slid from under her covers. In just a minute, she was out of her pajamas and into the white-and-orange dress she put on the tiny rocking chair next to her dresser. Neela opened the door to her bedroom and skipped down the carpeted hallway, stopping only to bang on her mom's bedroom door as she passed. Once in the kitchen, she pulled out the orange juice and poured two glasses, as well as placing four pieces of toast into the toaster (after moving one of the kitchen chairs up to the counter so she could reach). She ate her toast and flipped through pages of her mother's fashion magazine, just looking at the pictures of all the tall women with their glowing hair. A minute later, her mom strolled in. She was still in her own pajamas and was wiping away sleep dust from her eyes.

"Good morning, Mommy!" Neela said, walking over and handing her a plate with two pieces of dry toast on it. "I made you breakfast!"

Mommy smiled. "Aww, that's so sweet of you, Neela. Thank you. I'm not sure if I can eat all of this though!" she said, puffing out her cheeks and making a bloated face. Neela laughed.

"When you're done with your breakfast, can we go?" Neela asked.

"Oh, honey, the museum doesn't open until…"

"Nine!" Neela finished. "And it's eight-ten now, so we can finish breakfast. That should give you time to get dressed, find your repurpose items, and catch the tram to the museum. We should get there right at nine!" Neela said gleefully. Mommy could only laugh to herself and nod while eating her toast.

"Okay. Go get your repurpose items together, and we can go once I get dressed."

Neela beamed a huge smile, pushed herself away from the table, and ran down the hallway to her bedroom. There was a repurpose station outside the museum, so it would be easy for her and Mommy to drop off this month's items. Neela had collected a dress of hers that she liked but was rapidly outgrowing, as well as a box of new crayons she got for her birthday but did not need because she already had a box. She grabbed the two and raced back out to the kitchen.

Several minutes later, right on Neela's rigorous schedule, Mommy was strapping a pair of white sandals onto Neela's pink feet, and they were off to the tram station. Neela always liked the tram; it was quiet, and the cars all had huge, glass domes that let you watch all of the trees and parks rush past. Sitting on the tram looking out the window with the warm sun on her face made Neela start to feel drowsy, but just when it started to take hold, they pulled up to their stop, and Neela was energized with renewed vigor. She grabbed her mommy's hand and pulled her along to the front doors of the museum. As they approached, they passed the brightly painted red kiosk with the words "Repurpose" written in large white letters on all sides. Neela slid in her dress and box of crayons and watched as her mommy slid in a baking tray and several unused notebooks. Then it was off to the museum entrance, finally! When they approached, the familiar face of Constable Murphy met them by the front door. The constable looked down at Neela and smiled.

"Going to spend another day in our favorite place, little Ms. Neela?" asked the constable, bending down and placing his hands on his knees.

"I just turned twelve yesterday!" she said proudly.

The officer stood up and showed a surprised look on his face.

"Twelve years old already! Well now, I think that means something… What is it now? I can't seem to remember…" Constable Murphy said to the girl, placing his hand on his chin as he pondered.

"It means I can go into the grown-up section!" Neela responded.

"Oh, so it does! Well then, I better not keep you waiting," said the officer and stepped aside to let the two ladies through.

Once inside, Neela didn't bother with all of the exhibits she had already seen a dozen times; she knew what she came here for. She grabbed her mommy's hand and led her past the "Young Adults" section of the museum and past the double black doors that led to the adult sections. Once she approached the doors, the chip implanted in her neck at birth was read by the automatic scanners, revealing her to, in fact, be twelve years of age, and the doors opened for her and her mommy. Neela was amazed by all of the new items placed in brightly lit display cases or photos enlarged to be six feet high with paragraphs next to each one explaining its meaning and context. She would take her time to see all of these things soon enough, but there was one thing she always wanted to see, and it was this item that now sat in the center of the room. The case was small but brightly lit on the inside.

As Neela approached, she could see the soft velvet cushion inside, with a wooden stand in the middle. Neela went right up to the glass and stood on her tippy toes to get a better view of the item on the stand. It was a folded piece of paper that had been laid flat, the deep creases still clearly visible. Printed on the center of the paper was a painting of an ocean with a sunrise peering out from its horizon.

A brass plaque above the case had two words engraved on it: "Dia's Hope."

End

About the Author

Michael Deleo is a resident of suburban Philadelphia and an avid science, nature, and animal lover. When not storytelling, he can be found strolling around the many parks and lakes with his energetic dachshund Jim by his side. Michael also likes to spend his spare time building models, making dioramas, and cooking.

Printed in the USA
CPSIA information can be obtained
at www.ICGtesting.com
LVHW021618211124
797037LV00016B/985
* 9 7 9 8 8 9 3 0 8 3 3 1 6 *